The Laramie brothers are coming home to Lazy L....

The sun is shining down on Larch Valley as two ruggedly gorgeous brothers finally return home.

Their brooding good looks and troubled eyes may have all the local girls' hearts in a flutter, but these guarded men have turned their backs on romance....

See Drew put on his Stetson and take his childhood sweetheart in his arms for...

One Dance with the Cowboy
January 2010

And can war-weary hero Noah find someone to ease his pain and melt his frozen heart in

Her Lone Cowboy
March 2010

Wedding bells are ringing out in Larch Valley this New Year!

Dear Reader,

In 2008 our family moved from Alberta to the east coast of Canada. We left behind some very good friends but kept fond memories of the prairies. When I heard that my RWA chapter in Calgary was hosting a workshop, I knew I wanted to attend and reconnect. Around the same time I was doing some research on rescue ranches and came across the site for Bear Valley Rescue Ranch. I sent an e-mail, and it was returned with an invitation to visit.

So, when I attended the workshop in October, I also spent a sunny fall afternoon with Mike Bartley. He and his wife, Kathy, run Bear Valley, and I am so glad I went. Mike clearly believes in what he's doing and has a real affection for the animals—calling them sweetie and rubbing lots and lots of noses. We also visited the donated quarter section where he keeps most of the herd, and in that few moments a story blossomed.

Writing stories set in Larch Valley has been special because in a way it keeps me connected to the part of Canada I called home for over a decade. Little did I know when I wrote *The Rancher's Runaway Princess* how much I would look forward to visiting this town again. I hope you enjoy Jen and Andrew's story. Come back next month to meet Andrew's brother Noah and find out what happens when he meets the unstoppable Lily Germaine.

Until then,

Donna

DONNA ALWARD

One Dance with the Cowboy

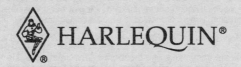

TORONTO • NEW YORK • LONDON
AMSTERDAM • PARIS • SYDNEY • HAMBURG
STOCKHOLM • ATHENS • TOKYO • MILAN • MADRID
PRAGUE • WARSAW • BUDAPEST • AUCKLAND

For John, Joyce, Gage and Dallas…we miss you.
Keep laughing.

Recycling programs
for this product may
not exist in your area.

ISBN-13: 978-0-373-17635-9

ONE DANCE WITH THE COWBOY

First North American Publication 2010.

Copyright © 2009 by Donna Alward.

A busy wife and mother of three (two daughters and the family dog), **Donna Alward** believes hers is the best job in the world: a combination of stay-at-home mom and romance novelist. An avid reader since childhood, Donna always made up her own stories. She completed her arts degree in English literature in 1994, but it wasn't until 2001 that she penned her first full-length novel and found herself hooked on writing romance. In 2006 she sold her first manuscript and now writes warm, emotional stories for the Harlequin® Romance line.

Now in her new home office in Nova Scotia, Donna loves being back on the east coast of Canada—after nearly twelve years in Alberta, where her career began—writing about cowboys and the West. Donna's debut, *Hired by the Cowboy,* was awarded the Booksellers Best Award in 2008 for Best Traditional Romance.

With the Atlantic Ocean only minutes from her doorstep, Donna has found a fresh take on life, and promises even more great romances in the near future!

Donna loves to hear from readers. You can contact her through her Web site at www.donnaalward.com, visit her MySpace page at www.myspace.com/dalward.

Happy New Year!

Welcome to 2010 and another year of fabulous, feel-good reads from Harlequin Romance.

This month, get swept up in *The Italian's Forgotten Baby* by **Raye Morgan.** An idyllic island and an irresistible Italian recapturing lost memories make for a real page-turner! Fasten your seat belt as your ESCAPE AROUND THE WORLD continues—on the arm of a gorgeous Mediterranean man in a hot-air balloon in sunny Spain! The warmth and emotion of **Barbara McMahon**'s *The Daredevil Tycoon* will leave your senses tingling!

If you'd rather keep your feet firmly on the ground perhaps you'll accept an invitation to the weddings of the year.... **Cara Colter** and **Shirley Jump** bring you *Just Married!*: two linked stories in one volume for double the chance to catch the bouquet!

After all that excitement, curl up and relax with a laid-back cowboy in **Donna Alward**'s heartwarming tale *One Dance with the Cowboy,* the first in her brand-new duet COWBOYS & CONFETTI. Then from the Rocky Mountains to the rolling hills of the English countryside, **Jessica Steele**'s perfect English gentleman will steal your heart in *The Girl from Honeysuckle Farm.*

If you love Jessica Steele, don't miss the warm, witty and wildly romantic *Hired: Sassy Assistant* by sparkling new talent **Nina Harrington.**

Which will you read first?

CHAPTER ONE

THERE were times in life you either had to go big, or go broke.

Jen's fingers paused on the pen, the cool tube turning warm and slippery in her hand as the room suddenly seemed hot and stifling. The loan papers sat before her and the numbers swirled in front of her eyes.

"Ms. O'Keefe?"

She looked up from the papers, her lightweight sweater cloying, the yellow silk scarf strangling her as her breath shallowed. It was such a *lot* of money, after all. The new bank manager's face frowned a little at her continued hesitation.

She took a breath, looked down, and signed her name—once, twice, three times.

She clicked the pen closed, feeling at once a euphoric blend of fear and excitement. Risk-taking was not her specialty. But over the years she'd learned it was a necessary evil at times. She'd run the numbers until she could cite them by rote. Everything she'd done told her this was a good move. A necessary move.

But seeing it in black and white, knowing that what she'd built so far could be swept away with one failure…it was enough to take a girl's breath away.

She would not hyperventilate. She would not.

She rose, shook the manager's hand. Not the same man who'd given her the first loan for Snickerdoodles; he'd been a friend of her father's and had retired last year. This man was in his late thirties, still exuding that air of big city rather than small town. It wasn't the same. It didn't give her the sense of security that she could really use right now.

Snickerdoodles Bakery was about to be transformed into Snickerdoodles Café and Catering, and if she'd miscalculated she'd lose it all.

"Congratulations, Ms. O'Keefe."

"Thanks." She smiled thinly, extricating her hand from his clasp. Watched as he slid her copy of the papers into a portfolio, handing it to her with a smile.

"Let us know if you need anything at all," he suggested, and she picked up her bag.

Need anything? There were enough zeroes on the dotted line that she hoped she wouldn't need a single thing more…ever.

She was nearly to the glass doors when the nerves hit full force.

She'd done it. She'd just remortgaged everything she had— including her house—to finance a complete refurbishment of her bakery.

She had to be crazy.

She scrambled to get outside, into some fresh air that might hold off the rising panic attack. If she could just get to one of the park benches lining Main Avenue she'd sit and put her head between her knees.

She pushed frantically through the doors, the vision of a bench swimming deliciously before her eyes. Except that halfway there her shoulder encountered a solid wall that took every last bit of oxygen from her lungs. The contact sent her staggering, the portfolio sliding out of her hands and skidding down the concrete sidewalk before coming to rest against a half-height barrel newly filled with petunias, lobelia, and some sort of trailing plant.

Warm, strong hands gripped her biceps, keeping her from falling on her rump in the middle of noon foot-traffic. She looked up, opened her mouth to speak, but instead fought to inhale now that the wind had been completely knocked out of her. Her mouth gaped and flapped as she fought for air to rush it back into her lungs. And if the jolt hadn't stolen her breath, the man attached to the hands definitely would have.

Finally blessed oxygen rushed in and she gasped. Her head tipped back as she looked way up into a too-familiar face. She saw the shock and confusion firing in his hazel eyes for just a moment, wondered if the same emotions were mirrored in her own. It seemed as if years of memories raced between them, though only a few seconds passed. His eyes cleared, cooled. Setting her firmly on her feet, he let her go briefly to retrieve her folder of papers and brought them back to her, holding them out as she fought to calm the hammering of her heart.

"Hello, Jen."

Somehow her hand slid out to take the folder from him, while the warm, slightly rough sound of his voice sank deep into her consciousness. His hands were gone from her arms now, and her skin felt cold in their absence, even though it was the first time he'd touched her in many, many years.

"Hello, Drew."

The moment she said it she felt the blush creeping up her neck, hoped that her scarf camouflaged her flushed skin. She'd been the only one ever to call him Drew. Everyone else had called him by his full name...Andrew. Not Andy, or any other shortened version. Drew had been saved just for her. They both knew it. And Jen saying it now had suddenly transported them to a place deep in the past. Somewhere she hadn't ever wanted to go again. Self-conscious, she raised one trembling hand to smooth the tendrils of hair that were escaping what had been her attempt at a sophisticated twist. When she realized what she was doing, she dropped her hand abruptly. She didn't need to preen for Andrew Laramie.

"Are you okay?"

She looked up into his mossy-gold eyes again, tucked the portfolio under an arm and resisted the urge to straighten her white sweater and matching skirt. *What are you doing here? Why are you back? How long are you staying?* All those questions raced through her mind, but she would not ask any of them—not after the way he'd treated her the last time he'd been home. The rebuff still stung. The answers shouldn't matter anyway. It was a public street. He had as much a right to be in Larch Valley as anyone. He owned half of the Lazy L Ranch, and everyone knew it. Just as they knew the place had been abandoned for the better part of a year.

"I'm fine, thank you." She brushed a hand down her skirt, simply to be doing something other than gawping at his too-handsome face.

"You're pale. Are you feeling all right?" He peered closer, his eyes clouded with concern.

The question erased the panicky thoughts about her bakery and a flash of annoyance flickered through her. What right did he have to worry about her now? None!

"I'm not one of your horses you can doctor, Andrew." This time she made sure she used his full first name. She adopted the most aloof expression she could and stepped back, adjusting the strap of her bag on her shoulder. "What are you doing here, anyway? Shouldn't you be getting ready for the Derby or something? I'd think the racing season'd be keeping you mighty busy."

She knew she sounded obnoxious and wished she could

take back the words. It was petty and not her style. After all this time she shouldn't let him rattle her.

It was no secret in Larch Valley that Andrew Laramie had gone on to a sparkling career in veterinary medicine, working in the racing industry south of the border. His dad, for all their falling out, had been proud of him. He'd said so every time she'd gone to visit him. It was a low blow to throw it back at Andrew now, but she couldn't seem to help it now that she was face to face with him. Just seeing him, in the middle of town on a busy Monday afternoon, put her on the defensive.

Maybe when he'd been home for the funeral they might have talked, put things to rest. But he'd spurned any sort of conversation, deliberately ignoring her when she'd reached out to him, put her hand on his arm in sympathy. She had only wanted to help, but he'd barely acknowledged her presence, brushing by her after the final prayer with only a sidelong glance. It had confirmed the fact that she needed to stop making herself available for him to hurt her. Once had been more than enough. She tended to learn her lessons.

"I'm not working in Virginia any more."

That wasn't current news, and she struggled to hide her surprise. "Greener pastures?"

His gaze landed on her, the censure in it heavy, and she lifted her chin in response.

"The Jen I remember never copped an attitude."

"The Jen you remember was a long time ago." She said it quickly, doubting he knew how much she'd truly loved him back then.

His eyes softened, and he seemed almost resigned as he agreed. "Yes, she was. I'm sorry for that."

It was as if he knew exactly what she was thinking—he'd always had an uncanny knack for it, and the last thing she wanted from him was understanding. Not now. What was he sorry for? His remark? Or a whole lot more? The fact that she wanted to know was frightening enough, and sent up a warning siren. *No.* She had to get out of here. Whatever had brought him to Larch Valley, she was sure something more important would take him right back out again. He was probably out to sell the ranch. Goodness knows he didn't need it or want it. He never had. She'd seen how his determination to stay away had hurt his father; it had hurt *her*, knowing he had turned his back on all of them. Now he could pocket all his lovely money and keep on with his oh-so-important career.

"I should get back. I have work to do," she said, aiming for polite civility. She should just go her own way and get on with things, as she'd been doing for several years now.

"Me too," he replied, but his gaze still held hers trapped within it. He lifted his hand and she froze as one long finger tucked a stray strand of hair behind her ear. Goosebumps erupted down her arms, shivering against the cool early spring air.

Then he stood back, tucking his hands into his jeans pockets. "I'll see you around, Jen."

He went past her, continuing west on Main Avenue, while she was left standing in the middle of the concrete sidewalk. She highly doubted she'd see him again when all was said and done.

She straightened her sweater and squared her shoulders. Today was one of those freak encounters, nothing more. Tomorrow she'd still be here, and he'd be gone.

As she pointed her white pumps toward her bakery, a block away, she reminded herself that leaving was what Andrew did best.

This time wouldn't be any different.

"Andrew. Gosh, it's good to see you!"

Andrew smiled, and it felt good. But it was impossible not

to smile at the red-haired pregnant woman coming down the steps toward him. He gave her a hug, and then set her back.

"Damn, you look good, Luce."

"You too. And you remind me of home. Well, the old home anyway."

He laughed at her impish expression. He'd met Lucy many years ago when he'd done some work at Trembling Oak and she'd barely been out of high school. When he'd been back late last fall he'd realized she was the one his good friend Brody had e-mailed about, and that she was a real, bona-fide princess. He'd nearly fallen off his chair.

But it was good to see she hadn't changed. And it was great to know Brody was so happy.

"It's good to be back," he said, looking up at the farmhouse, and he discovered he meant it.

"Come on in. Mrs. Polcyk's made a streusel cake and there's a pot of coffee on. Brody'll be back soon, and you can tell us about your plans."

He followed her into the house.

The first thing that greeted him was the scent, and he was reminded not of his own house, at Lazy L, but the afternoons he'd spent at the O'Keefes'. Molly O'Keefe had been a hell of a baker; where Jen inherited it from, he supposed. He'd always felt more at home there than he had at his own place, with just his dad and his brother Noah for company.

"Well, Andrew Laramie. If this isn't a touch of the prodigal coming home."

He struggled not to blush as Betty Polcyk rounded the cupboard and enfolded him in a hug.

"Hi, Betty."

"It's about time you got yourself back here."

"Yes'm." He'd learned long ago that no one argued with Mrs. Polcyk.

"Sit down. I'll get you some cake and coffee. Brody's on his way in too."

Slices of cinnamony cake were procured, along with coffee for Andrew and a large glass of milk for the pregnant Lucy. He'd taken his first meltworthy bite when the door slammed and Brody came in.

Andrew rose to meet his old friend and the two shook hands. Brody hadn't changed. Slightly older than Andrew, but still with the ready smile Andrew remembered, still big as a barn door, and still the kind of man who could be counted on. Andrew hoped he could count on him now.

"Good to see you, Brody."

"You too. Good to have you back." He went to the sink, washed his hands, and took a chair at the table as Andrew resumed his seat. "I was nearly thinking about making an offer on Lazy L if you hadn't shown your face around here again. But I figured you and Noah'd have to work it out first."

"I've bought him out."

The words hurt a little. Noah hadn't put up an argument, and Andrew knew the cash from the sale would be a nice addition to Noah's wages as a soldier. It was the fact that it had had to be done that had bothered Andrew. He hadn't been ready for the old man to go. But there was no changing it now. The important thing was that Lazy L was his.

"Hadn't heard that part."

"Half a ranch isn't doing him much good when he's overseas. I'm here to ask for some help."

Brody sipped his coffee while Lucy put down her fork. "What sort of help?"

"I'm using the land to start up a rescue ranch."

Brody's cup went back to the table and Andrew met his gaze squarely. He knew it wasn't what Brody had expected to hear. But Andrew knew it was what he wanted to do. Needed to do.

"There's no money in that, Andrew. How're you going to live?"

This part, at least, was the part he'd figured out. "What I've put by will keep things afloat. I'm taking the front third of the barn and converting it into a small clinic. There's no mortgage on the place, and I'll make enough to support myself. I've got a good reputation as a vet. I'm counting on word getting around that I'm back in business."

"And the horses you take in...no vet bills will be a help?"

"Yes."

Lucy folded her hands. "Still a lot of work. A lot of money for upkeep. And a big change for you."

It *was* a big change, and he knew it must sound and look odd. The truth was he was burnt out. He'd gotten the career he'd wanted but he'd tired of it. It wasn't all it seemed, and he'd seen more than he cared to. Had compromised his principles a few too many times to hold on to his self-respect. He swallowed, remembering the day he'd made the decision to walk away from it all. It had felt good, right. He'd bought out Noah's half of Lazy L and still had more than enough to sustain himself—thanks to some savvy financial decisions along the way.

He could afford to do this, but he wanted help. He wanted it to be bigger than the sum of its parts. He wanted it to be not only about him, but something that was meaningful to the community. The trouble was doing it now, when everyone knew he'd turned his back on Larch Valley and the people in it a long time ago.

"I've been away for years. What I need to do is build goodwill again. Memories are long, and people remember that I left and didn't come back." He thought of Jen, thought of his father, and both left an ache in his chest. His father was gone; it was too late to mend fences. But Jen was still here.

Even if she acted like she hated him, he knew he had to try to make amends. Somehow.

"I thought…in a few weeks…when I get the house and barns sorted a bit, I could throw a bit of a benefit. Maybe a dance like your Dad used to throw in the summers—remember, Brody?"

Brody and Lucy shared a long, tender look. "It's still an annual event," Lucy said softly, and Brody's fingers came to link with hers.

Andrew stared at their joined hands, thinking of Jen again. There had been a time when they'd held hands constantly, naively thinking everything would be easy and glorious and perfect. How wrong they'd been. Seeing her at the funeral had been a blow, a reminder of his many failures when it came to people who mattered. He hadn't known what to say, had been so bound up in his grief that he'd been sure he'd get it all wrong. And yesterday on the street she'd made it very clear his presence wasn't welcomed. He was honest enough with himself to admit it had stung a little. He had told himself not to expect her to welcome him back with open arms, but he'd thought she'd be a little more civil. Jen had always been understanding and open.

But he'd worry about that later. Right now, it was all about picking Brody and Lucy's brains about holding a benefit.

"I was thinking you two would know who I should ask… who to hit up for donating time or materials. I'd like community involvement to keep the ranch sustainable. Frankly, it's more about awareness than it is about the money."

Brody nodded. "I'll make a list…suppliers and farmers who'd be willing to donate feed and hay. Ranchers in the area, for sure. Local farriers, and definitely local media." Brody looked at Lucy. "Media might best be handled by you, don't you think?"

"I'll polish up the tiara," she quipped. "And I'll help with the party end too, Andrew, if I can. You'll need music and decorations—we'll get those donated, never fear—and food."

Andrew felt himself get swept up in the whirlwind of planning, realizing that he was actually doing this. He was throwing away his illustrious career in order set up an operation that wouldn't make him any profit. He had to be crazy. And yet for the first time in years he felt energized, excited. As if he were doing something worthwhile. Something bigger than himself.

"Food? What sort of food?" He knew Betty always did a huge spread for the Hamilton Barn Dance, but he wouldn't presume to ask her. "A barbecue?"

"No, I don't think so. Nights are still pretty chilly, and who's going to want to stand outside for that? I think you need finger foods, buffet-style." Lucy winked at him. "And these are ranchers. So none of those canapés and pâtés you and I are used to, hmmm?"

He laughed. It was good to come home and be welcomed. He hoped that by throwing this party more doors would open up for him. People tended to have long memories in small towns. Up until now it hadn't really mattered.

"Well, I'm sure not able to cook it. Who do you suggest?"

"Jen O'Keefe."

His grin froze. Brody barked out a laugh. "Nice one, honey," he chuckled.

"Did I say something wrong?"

"I saw Jen yesterday," Andrew replied acidly. "She'd rather poison me, I think." Poison. Hah! Of all the townspeople, Jen would probably be the hardest to win over.

"Jen's sweet," Lucy defended loyally. "She'd never poison anyone."

Andrew shook his head. "Oh, yes, she would, and I'd be top of her list."

"Whatever for? You just arrived."

That's right, he had. But before that he'd gone, and he hadn't kept his promise. She hated him and she had every reason.

"Because I'm an idiot, Lucy." He accepted the words for what they were—the truth. "She'll never agree, anyway. She doesn't even want to look at me, let alone allow me to hire her for some shindig. And doesn't she own the bakery?"

Lucy nodded, running a finger along her bottom lip. "Yes, but she was going to see the bank about a loan to expand. She's branching out into catering. Oh, it's perfect, Andrew. She'll be closed while renovations are ongoing. In the meantime she can cater for you, and it'll be advance advertising for her new venture."

It made sense. If it were anyone but Jen. But yesterday she'd looked at him as if he was dirt beneath her shoes. She'd been coming out of the bank...had she got her loan?

"She's a brilliant cook."

"I remember," he said without thinking.

Lucy raised an eyebrow.

Brody nudged her. "They go *way* back."

Andrew shook his head. "Don't get any ideas, Lucy. Whatever was between Jen and me has been over for a long time. And it'll stay over if yesterday is any indication." He ignored the twinge of regret he felt at saying the words. "The only way she'll agree is if maybe you ask her. She won't even speak to me." If he were going to mend fences he was going to have to take his time. Asking her for a favor wasn't going to put him in her good books.

But Lucy shook her head. "No way, buster. I'm not being a go-between. Time to grow up. Imagine a party and you saying *Tell Jen that I said...* and her answering with *Tell Andrew that I said...*" She set her jaw. "This isn't Junior High. Jen is the best person in this town to cater your party, and if you want her you're going to have to ask her yourself. Otherwise you're going to end up at Ready-Right buying deli trays and potato chips."

They almost sounded appetizing compared to having to face Jen's coldness and ask her to take the job. Eating crow had never been his favorite menu item.

But the bigger picture was making his objective a success and putting his best foot forward. And cubed cheese and crackers wasn't going to do that.

He was going to have to ask her. And she'd either say yes or no. One thing he knew for sure. He wouldn't beg.

CHAPTER TWO

SNICKERDOODLES BAKERY lay in the middle of Main Avenue, a two story plain building painted brick-red and with the false front found on many of the other buildings gracing the quaint street. Its western character was part of what Jen loved about Larch Valley—the sense of timelessness and comfort that came with it. It was a town with heart, with soul, with family. And even though her parents had retired nearby, in the more convenient city of Lethbridge, Jen had made the decision to stay.

The truth was, she didn't want to let go of it. Nor did she want to let go of the business she'd built from scratch—much like the way she built her cakes and pies and breads. It hadn't taken long after Ready-Right built their store for Jen's business to suffer. She could either let it go, or decide to take a risk.

She'd risked. And, despite the moments of panic, it felt right.

But today, pasting the announcement in her front window, it seemed rather daunting.

After her bank meeting last Monday she'd met with the contractors, and then had spent the remainder of her afternoon poring over catalogs. New equipment, new furniture. New signage. And closing for nearly a month to make it all happen.

Yup. Definitely certifiable, she thought, turning over the "open" sign and unlocking the door. In a few days the ovens would be cool and this door would remain closed. But for today she'd take pleasure in baking her favorites.

It was a warm morning, and she opened the inside door, nudging in a stopper with her toe and letting the spring air through the wood-framed screen. She smiled as she went back to the kitchen to finish cooking the filling for date squares. The screen door would also let the smell of her fresh baking out…the best and cheapest form of advertising she knew.

She'd just slid the tray of squares into the convection oven and set the timer when she heard the slap of the screen door against the frame.

She wiped her hands on her cobbler's apron and left the hot kitchen, going into the main part of the bakery, cool with the breeze wafting in. She paused when she saw the tall figure standing next to a rack lined with fresh bread loaves. This made twice that he'd appeared this week, and each time her breath had caught at the sight of him. She resolutely pushed the reaction to one side, and reminded herself that he had been the one to walk away.

"Still here, then?"

He turned, and her heart stuttered in her chest.

She'd already seen him once; the shock of their eyes meeting should have been over. But it wasn't. Seeing him today, a brown Stetson on his head, his hazel eyes shining at her from within his tanned face, had the power to reach inside her and take hold. It was as if no time had passed at all and he was standing before her ready to ask if she'd like to go for a ride in his truck. The memory ached with sweetness.

It was a physical reaction, but it came from a heart that had never quite forgotten what it was like to be loved by him.

"I'm still here."

"Why?"

It struck her as odd that they dispensed with any pleasantries. No *good morning* or *what brings you back*? or even a polite *how are you*? Perhaps they were past the need for small talk. Perhaps they were past the need to pretend for each other. Either way, neither of them tried to make the meeting something it wasn't. He was here. She wanted to know why.

He stepped forward, his hands in the pockets of his brown farm jacket. The counter separated them; Jen was glad of it. He couldn't see how her fingers were fussing with the display case between them.

"I'm staying at Lazy L."

"You are?" He was out at his old farmhouse? But it had been vacant for six months—longer if you counted the time his father had been in the hospital. It could hardly be suitable for visitors.

"For good."

Those two words sucked the wind clear out of her sails. Dealing with Andrew being in town for a few days was one thing. Knowing he was going to be back here indefinitely was quite another.

It would be a daily reminder. It wasn't something she could just put in a box for a finite amount of time and forget about once he was gone again.

"What about your career?" The words felt strangled, coming out of her mouth dry with nervousness.

"My career has taken a different path."

She didn't know what to say. Any response she might have thought of left her head as he slowly lifted his hand and removed his hat.

His hair was short, the tawny strands just long enough for a girl to run her fingers through. While the Stetson had shadowed his eyes a bit, they now glowed the color of the timothy he'd used to pick for her—the kind they'd chewed between their teeth as they'd walked the fields west of town, going nowhere.

"What sort of different path? You never wanted the farm," she said softly. *Never wanted to be tied here*, she remembered. But the last thing she wanted to do was bring up their old history. She'd thought enough about it last night, tossing and turning until past midnight.

"I never wanted what my father had laid out for me. You know that," he answered. "But it doesn't matter now. I'm back, and I'm starting up a rescue ranch."

She wanted to know more. She wanted to ask him why now, why here. What had changed. But seeing him brought back a lot of old feelings that had already taken a long time to get past. Hurt, for one. Learning not to love him so much. And anger. She'd done a lot of being angry and she didn't want to do it again. It was a life-sucking emotion, and she needed all her energy over the next few months to restructure her business.

She was a girl who learned her lessons.

"Could you come out from behind there so we can talk properly?"

She swallowed, forced her fingers to still. Andrew Laramie had broken her heart over a decade before, and he wouldn't do it again. They'd find a way to coexist in this town, and she'd make peace, but that would be the end of it.

"No, I don't think so."

"Jen…"

She raised a hand, closing her eyes. "Don't say my name that way."

And suddenly she was aware that they both knew nothing was over. No matter what lies they'd been telling themselves.

Silence reigned for a few moments and Jen opened her eyes. He was still there, still waiting. Not disappearing. She wished he would. After so many months of wanting him to come back, she now wished he'd go away and take his complication with him.

"Do you want to talk about this, Jen? Because we never did, and—"

"No, I don't." She said the words strongly. She'd lived through it once. She couldn't survive it again.

His eyes cooled as he rested back on his heels. "I deserve that." He pulled a newspaper clipping from his pocket. "You read this week's paper?"

"Not yet. Why?"

He handed her the clipping and stepped back. She scanned the first paragraph and looked up. "A charity benefit?"

"Lucy works fast. I didn't expect to get any publicity so soon."

"You know Lucy?" This was rapidly growing bigger than she could have imagined. It almost felt as if he was coming in and hijacking her life—which was silly. She'd built a life, one without him in it, just the way he'd wanted.

"I met her in Virginia several years ago. And I've asked Brody for his help too."

She looked down at the picture of Andrew; it was a stock photo that had been taken a few years ago at Churchill Downs, when a prominent racehorse had been injured. He'd certainly chased his dream and found it, but now it appeared he'd paid a price for it. So had she. He couldn't expect her to forget it with a pair of gorgeous eyes and a smile.

"I still don't know what you're doing here, Andrew, so why don't you get to the point?"

He cleared his throat. "The point is, I need someone to cater the food for the benefit. And Lucy insisted on you."

Lucy insisted. Not his idea at all. She felt the wisp of gratitude for her friend's loyalty quickly overshadowed by an irrational annoyance at Andrew's ambivalence. "Meaning *you* would have gone with someone else?"

"I didn't say that." He started tapping his hand against his thigh. Swept it out to the side in an encompassing gesture. "*This* is why I didn't want to ask. I didn't want it to be awkward, or...or difficult."

She softened the slightest bit. "What else could it be after all this time?"

For a long moment their gazes caught, and in his she sensed apology. She had never been one to hold a grudge. Yet at the same time every nerve-ending within her warned her to protect herself. She would always have a weak spot for Andrew.

"Lucy said you were the right one for the job. And I trust her judgment."

He trusted Lucy, but not her. She lifted her chin a little. She wasn't sure what she'd expected. She *wanted* him to keep his distance. It didn't make sense for her to be the least bit wounded by the fact that she hadn't been *his* choice.

"I'm sorry, Andrew, but I'll be in the middle of renovations here." She pointed at the sign in the front window announcing her temporary closure.

"Which is why it's the perfect time." He stepped forward. "I understand you're branching out into a café, and a catering side business. What better way to get a head start than by catering a job for me? You'll have positive publicity before you even open. It will give you something to do besides fret and drive the workmen crazy." He grinned at her disarmingly and she caught herself nearly smiling back.

She aimed him what she hoped was a look laced with skepticism. It wouldn't do to admit it, but the idea *was* sound. If he was already getting coverage in the local paper, then she *could* readily promote the new business before her grand reopening. She shouldn't turn it down just because it was Andrew doing the hiring. Surely she had more business sense than that?

"I'll think about it." She delivered what she hoped was the

world's most impersonal smile. But then he smiled back, wide and unreserved, and it lit up the room.

"I'd forgotten how you could do that," he chuckled. "Look, I'd have invited you anyway, Jen. The Christensen Brothers are playing, and heck, half the town and then some are coming. You'd be helping me and I'd be helping you."

"I don't want your help."

"Maybe I want to give it anyway. I owe you." He took a step forward, closer to the glass case that separated them, close enough that she could see the tiny wrinkles at the corners of his eyes. He looked tired.

She knew it shouldn't make a whit of difference to her.

He'd never needed her; he'd made that abundantly clear. She turned away as the oven timer went off, went to slide the squares out of the oven and onto a rack to cool. When she turned around he'd come through to the back and stood in the door to her kitchen. The screen door slapped again and she was trapped; she would have to pass by him to reach the storefront.

"You don't owe me anything," she said quietly.

"Maybe I want to make amends, too," he said quietly.

"Isn't it a little late for that?" She whispered it, torn between wanting to reach out and bridge the gap between them and wanting him to simply go away and let her get on with the life she'd built without him.

"Come out to Lazy L. It's not all done yet, but come out anyway. See what I'm doing. See if you don't believe in it. If you turn down the job after the tour, I'll accept it. I promise. Just give me a chance."

Promises were exactly what she wanted to avoid when it came to Andrew Laramie, but she heard the ding of the silver bell next to the cash register and heaved a sigh of frustration. She couldn't keep whoever it was out there waiting forever.

"Why does it matter to you what I think? I'd just be the caterer."

He looked her in the eye. "It matters. It's always mattered."

Her heart stuttered at that pronouncement just for a second. But the rustle of her customer picking up merchandise jolted it back to a regular rhythm and she knew she had to get a move on. "Fine. I'll come out for a tour. On Sunday. Now, will you let me get back to work?"

He stepped aside as she hustled out to the front, pasting on a smile for the customer who had come in.

She was making change when he came out of the kitchen behind her. Agnes Dodds from the antiques shop up the street snapped her eyes open as he passed, but that wasn't what got to Jen.

He'd put his hat back on, and as he went behind her to reach the door his hand ever so lightly grazed her waist, lingering for a second, before he turned the corner and shouldered his way out the door.

Try as she might to forget it, the band of skin where he'd touched her burned with remembrance for the rest of the morning. She'd go see the ranch. And she'd decide about catering. But whatever else Andrew had in mind was strictly off-limits.

The foothills were beginning to green up after the spring rain when Jen made the drive out to the Lazy L Ranch for the first time in months. The ruts in the dirt road leading to the farmhouse were different, but so many things remained unchanged that for a few moments she suffered a distinct feeling of déjà-vu.

Andrew spoke of making amends. She wasn't sure what to make of that. A lot of time had passed, and she'd spent a good part of it putting their relationship behind her. She wasn't even sure she was interested in *amends* when it had been so difficult to reach *acceptance*. Maybe this was what he needed to make it okay for himself. Maybe she should listen to what he had to say. She didn't have any desire to hurt him, after all. Maybe hearing him out would be best, and then they could both move on and the ridiculous flutterings that happened when she was near him would disappear for good.

She pulled up in front of the house and parked next to a new pick-up truck—a shiny red diesel with enough power to haul a good-sized trailer, like the one parked next to the barn. The house itself looked lonely. The paint on the porch was peeling, the front door was faded from years of sun and wind. The corral beside the barn was empty, a few of the railings broken and drooping.

He had his work cut out for him.

She got out of her car and immediately heard the sound of hammering coming from the barn. She followed the noise, taking in the brown dry grass of the previous fall that had never been trimmed. It seemed things had fallen by the wayside here even before Gerald's death. If Andrew was planning on holding a dance here in a few weeks he had a lot to do.

She found him in the barn. It had been swept clean, and he was working in a T-shirt and jeans, with a stack of two-by-fours and one-by-sixes by his feet as he repaired broken boards. A brown tool belt hung low at his hips, accentuating the curve of his bottom as he reached down for the lumber. Dust motes swam in the beams of sunlight as he raised the hammer and nailed a board into place, the muscles in his shoulders and back plainly revealed through the cotton tee. Instead of his Stetson today, he wore a ball cap, and she could see the precise line where his hair met his neck, neatly trimmed. She had the absurd urge to run her finger along the shorn edge.

The house was a derelict, and there wasn't a lick of hay in

the place, and yet he was determined to accomplish this. She couldn't help but be impressed by his dedication alone. It echoed back to what she herself was trying to achieve—how could she in turn discourage him?

"Andrew?"

He whirled at the sound of her voice and she tried a smile. "I told you I'd come. But if you're too busy…"

"Of course not." He put down his hammer and unhooked the belt, the nails in the pouch jangling as he put it on the floor beside the neat lengths of wood. "Your timing is fine. I was going to take a break for a drink anyway."

His boots made hollow noises on the bare floor as he made his way over to where she stood. "Excuse the mess. Things are in a bit of disrepair, as you can see."

"I didn't know…"

"Neither did I. I should have. I realize that now." He gestured toward the ladder. "I didn't think you'd come, though I hoped you would. I've got a cooler downstairs with some drinks. I'll give you the grand tour—what there is of it."

She went down the ladder ahead of him, and was treated to a tempting view of his backside as he followed. There was no denying the physical attraction still existed. He had lost the callowness of youth and grown into himself. She'd always found him handsome, and it was just her dumb luck that he was even more so now. But she'd learned the hard way that it certainly wasn't enough to pin a girl's hopes on.

She looked away and followed him down the corridor to what was meant to be a tackroom. It still housed a few old saddles and bridles, but they, like the rest of Lazy L, hadn't been cared for in quite some time. The leather looked faded and cracked.

He opened a small cooler and handed her a can. She popped the top, all the while aware that it was just the two of them out here in the relative middle of nowhere. The isolation of it lent itself to a certain intimacy. He cracked his own top and took a long swallow, his throat bobbing three times before he lowered the can. A small trickle of sweat gleamed at his right temple.

A bird sang outside in the wild rose bushes.

She lowered her can. He lowered his. And for a heart-stopping moment everything held, waiting, waiting. His gaze dropped to her lips and a rush of warmth flooded her body. All it would take was one step by either of them and...

And it was exactly what she didn't want. Her eyes flickered away. It was only the memory of this exact spot, the place where they'd first kissed all those years ago. It did something to her, pulled her in. She needed to remember she was here as a businesswoman.

"How about that tour?"

Andrew put the can down on a dusty ledge and she froze as he stepped nearer. Her words had been steady but her heart was a traitor as it sped up at the proximity of his body to hers. She kept walking backward but misjudged, and her back found solid wall.

"A...Andrew." She stuttered his name as he took the can from her hands and put it down. "Don't do this."

He took her cold hands in his warm ones and searched her eyes. The low peak of his cap shaded the upper half of his face, darkly mysterious in the dim light of the tackroom. Their first kiss. She remembered it as if it was yesterday. The nervous tumbling in her stomach, the excitement, the naked yearning. What she'd thought were resolutions suddenly didn't seem so resolved anymore. All those feelings and more were the ones she was feeling *right now*.

His thumbs rubbed over the tops of her hands. "Don't do what?"

Kiss me, she thought, but pursed her lips together. She wouldn't say it. Wouldn't voice it. She'd long ago promised herself she'd never ask him for anything ever again. Along with the flare of attraction she felt the knife-sharp edge of pain—how she'd felt the moment she'd accepted he was not coming back. No, he couldn't kiss her again. Not now. She turned her head away, but he released one hand, reaching up to grip her chin and turning it back to face him.

Andrew looked into her eyes, so dark a blue they were almost black in the muted light. He was touching her again, her icy hand in his, her perfect chin cupped within his fingers. He wanted to kiss her. Wanted to taste her lips beneath his and see if they still tasted the same. If she still made that breathy sigh she always had when he'd touched the delicate corner of her mouth with his own. Wanted to know so badly that he nearly forgot why he'd asked her here.

And she was wondering too. He could see it in the way her chest rose and fell, almost frantically, the way her pupils dilated when he moved in a couple of inches.

And then he closed his eyes and heard the words he'd never been able to get out of his head. *"You owed us better."*

It hadn't been Jen who had said them, but she'd been included in the sentiment, and he knew now that Gerald Laramie had been right. What he owed Jen now was an added complication. He needed to somehow make it up to her. He'd been a coward for a long time. What he wanted to do now was show her the man he'd become. He wasn't proud of all the decisions he'd made along the way. He was proud, however, of what he meant to do *from this day onward*. And for some reason her stamp of approval was worth something.

"Jen," he said softly, shocked to see the glimmer of tears in her eyes as he held her chin. Dear God, had he done that to her? Was it possible she still cared for him? After all this time? Or had he hurt her that much?

Leaving her had been harder than she realized, but there'd been so much more going on at the time he hadn't known what else to do. He'd been eighteen, and faced with a burden he hadn't expected. He'd had dreams, hopes, but ones she hadn't shared. Coming back to Larch Valley had been impossible that first year, and had grown more difficult each year since as his pride got in the way. It had only been when Gerald had died last fall that he'd realized he'd let it go too long.

He cleared his throat, released her. "We made so many mistakes," he conceded. "I won't compound them today. It's just…seeing you after all this time. It brings back a lot of memories."

He couldn't help but admire her backbone as she straightened, her shoulders back and tall with confidence.

"You either give me the tour and try to convince me to cater your dance, or you get out of my way and let me leave." She tried to sound strong but the words came out with a distinct wobble. "This…" she waved her finger between the two of them, speaking more clearly "…won't happen."

Her flat denial grated on his pride.

"Even if you want it to?"

He hadn't been wrong about the longing in her eyes, about the way their bodies seemed to gravitate together without even trying. He wasn't immune either. He remembered their first kiss in this very room. The way she'd been joking around, sitting on a saddle, and he'd pulled her off into his arms. They'd been in a cocoon of privacy in the barn, and he'd been sure she could hear his heart beating through his chest.

Like it was right now.

"I don't want it."

He backed off. He didn't either. Not really. He wanted to

start out on a new foot, not work backward. But he tended to forget his intentions the moment he saw the flush on her creamy skin, or the way two tendrils of hair always seemed to escape her ponytail and frame her face.

He gave her space to move, and move she did. She slid out around him and out the tackroom door into the main barn area.

He followed closely behind, watching her dark ponytail swing as she strode away. He knew two things for sure at that moment. Firstly, his intentions had been honorable. He did want to set things right between them. And secondly, honorable intentions didn't always work out the way one hoped.

Because he still wanted to kiss her. And he had no idea what to do about it.

CHAPTER THREE

THE air outside the tackroom was blessedly cool and Jen inhaled several times, trying to slow her pulse. She shouldn't let him get to her. She shouldn't let memories of the two of them have any power. What she needed to be doing was focusing on how she was going to improve her business. The money she'd make catering this function would help carry her through the month she was closed, giving her a head start in paying back her loan. It would give her a chance to promote early. Summer was coming up. There were any number of functions she could cater: showers and weddings and family picnics. So she'd just ignore Andrew's hazel eyes and stay on course. For all she knew he'd play at this awhile and then be gone as fast as he'd arrived. But for now she'd play along.

"We've got room for several horses in here, if we need it, to house them in cold weather." His voice came from behind her, strong but somewhat mollified, and she was relieved that he wasn't going to pursue what had just happened between them. It was just old history creating atmosphere. It wasn't real—couldn't be. It would be much better if they stuck to business.

His boots echoed on the concrete, the sound ricocheting through the empty barn. "I'm taking the front quarter of the barn and adding a clinic. I've got some men coming over this week to do the building, and I've got equipment and supplies on order. I'll be able to doctor my own stock, as well as that of other ranchers in the area."

She stopped at the last stall and put her hand on the door, turning to face him now that she was back in control of her emotions. "You shouldn't have much problem with drumming up business once word gets around."

But for how long? He was prominent, successful. How long before he got bored with Lazy L and Larch Valley and went back to his real life?

"That is the hope." He nodded. "I can manage financially without it, but I don't think I'd feel like me if I weren't practicing, you know?"

It was surprising to realize he was financially secure at such a young age. Goodness, he was so much more sure of himself than he'd used to be, and it was a little intimidating—especially considering she was barely scraping by and had just gone into debt so substantially. "If you enjoy practice so much, then why come back? Why now? You were so successful in the States. Your dad was always talking about you."

His head snapped up, his gaze catching hers, and she thought she detected a flare of pain before it was quickly doused.

"My father?"

She wasn't sure how to answer the clipped question; clearly the mention of Gerald put Andrew on edge. She decided to tread carefully. "I used to visit him after you left. Take him cookies. He followed your career from the start, you know."

It had been hard for Jen, hearing all about the life Andrew had chosen instead of choosing her. But Gerald had been good to her, and she knew he had been lonely. It had always been clear to her that Gerald had been as hurt about Andrew's severing of ties as she had. They had had that in common, and when Noah had been deployed Jen had started taking treats to the older man every few weeks or so. Over the years she'd seen him less and less. That had all changed when he had been taken to hospital. Then Jen hadn't been able to stand to see the aging man alone, when his sons couldn't be bothered to come see him.

Andrew shook his head, as if he didn't quite believe her. "No, I didn't know that. He never told me."

Andrew gestured forward and they exited out into the bright spring light, walking toward the corral by tacit agreement. He seemed reluctant to spend any more words on his father, so Jen decided to try talking about the ranch and his project again.

"So why here, and why now?"

They ambled slowly while a red-winged blackbird flitted from bush to bush ahead of them. "The racing world isn't all glory," he said finally. "Ask Lucy. She saw lots at Trembling Oak, and it's one of the better places I've been. I grew tired of watching it all. Horses bred to excess and then disposed of when they're not profitable. It's that elephant in the room that no one wants to discuss, you know? The world only really sees the glamorous side. And it's certainly not limited to the racing industry by any means. It's everywhere."

He sighed. "There are no easy answers or quick fixes." He leaned against the fence surrounding the corral. "I didn't mean to jump on my soap box. I guess it just ate away at me a little more each day until I knew I had to get out." He sighed. "There came a time when it seemed like I was helping take more lives than I was saving. It eats away at a man. I wanted to do something more positive."

"So now you're trying to change the world? It's a big step, Andrew. Some would say foolish."

"Change the world? Hardly. Change *my* world, definitely. Maybe it's selfish of me to retreat to some quiet corner of land rather than get out there and beat a drum."

"People handle things in different ways. It doesn't make them right—or wrong either." Who was she to judge? She'd made her own decisions and she'd lived with them. Tried not to regret them, or second-guess herself. She looked out over the empty corral, wondering what it would look like filled with horses, as it had been once before.

"So what did it for you? What was the moment you knew you wanted out?"

Once she'd said them, the words were like a knife with two edges, echoing back to that September morning when he'd gone away to school, never to come back. He'd promised he'd return. That she'd never be alone. She'd never understood why he hadn't at least offered an explanation.

Andrew picked at a splinter on the corral railing. "I put down a yearling simply because he wasn't going to be profitable for the racing operation. A beautiful, gorgeous sorrel." He turned, looked into her eyes, and once again she felt the jolt of awareness that somehow had never quite gone away.

"I cried, Jen. I did it, and I cried over that horse, and that's when I knew."

Her throat burned as she swallowed. There were times she wanted to find fault with him, to issue blame for how he'd hurt her. But not now, not at this moment. This moment all she felt was sorry, because it was obvious this was something that had touched him deeply.

"You did the right thing," was all she could say, but she wasn't at all sure. Because coming home to Larch Valley and Lazy L might not be the right thing at all. And then where would he go?

"I've had enough of the limelight. I made my money on the backs of those horses, Jen. Now maybe I can do something good with it. Find some peace of mind."

His impassioned words struck a chord with her. He'd

always had such ambition. Now that drive was tempered by compassion, and her resentment toward him began to thaw. Maybe he wasn't all about the glory and the money and the greener grass after all.

And then she remembered how he'd been too focused on building that illustrious career to visit his ailing father. And the truth of the matter was she was a long way from trusting that he wouldn't pull a disappearing act again. What was to say this wasn't just some transition period? What if he was just going through some sort of personal crisis?

"But there's just you here." She looked around, seeing the evidence of many months of neglect. It was a large job for one man, and lent itself to the notion that perhaps he hadn't thought it through as much as he ought to have. "You can't possibly do this all by yourself."

"I don't want it to be just me, though, don't you see?"

His eyes lit up—a distinct change from the gravity of moments ago.

"I could afford to run this on my own. But I don't want to. I want it to be bigger than me. That's why I want to involve local businesses. Let them contribute to it so it makes it a community effort. Feed, hay, fostering—heck, even just helping out with the day-to-day chores."

She could see how his plans energized him, once again making her feel she hardly knew him at all. Had she ever—truly?

He reached out and took her hand. "I felt good about it the moment my decision was made. And then I thought, why keep that to myself? What right have I to it? I wanted something good to finally come out of Lazy L. Who knows? Maybe Noah will come back for a while after his tour is over."

She left her hand in his for a few moments, not knowing what to say. Something good *had* come out of Lazy L—him.

Why couldn't he see it? Why did he run around chasing it? Frustration bubbled, but she had no idea what to say.

Why had he left it until now, when it was empty and abandoned? Gerald hadn't been able to keep it up either, and yet he'd refused to sell. He'd insisted the ranch be there for his boys. It was a sad thing when all was said and done. Noah didn't want his share and Andrew hadn't come home until Gerald had passed on. She wondered if that was on his list of regrets as well. She knew very well that Gerald would have backed his son in his project and been proud of it. He'd always been so proud.

"Do you ever wish you'd made other choices?"

Andrew let go of her hand. It felt too natural in his, and made him forget the reasons why he'd left her in the first place. He looked over at her, resting his arms on the top rail of the fence. The empty, dusty corral was before them. Other choices? He wasn't the second-guessing type. But seeing her these last few days, the beautiful woman that had grown out of the girl, he'd let himself wonder if all the years spent trying to prove himself had been worth it. In a way, she represented everything Larch Valley stood for. He wanted a chance to win her over, as he'd never been able to do with Gerald.

But he wasn't looking for a romantic attachment. Some things were meant to be left behind.

"I'm not in the habit of second-guessing myself," he remarked, knowing it wasn't entirely true. "If I'd made different choices I wouldn't be here now. And this is where I want to be. And what's the sense in wishing anyway? I can't change what I did. You don't get do-overs. You just make your decisions, hope they're the right ones, and get on with it."

He'd played the "what if?" game lots over the first few years he'd been gone. And he'd never received any good answers.

"But you learn from your mistakes...or at least a wise man

does," she replied. A breeze toyed with the hair next to her face, pinning a strand to the corner of her mouth. He watched, fascinated, as she hooked it with a finger and tucked it away. She'd been eighteen when he'd left Larch Valley for university, but he remembered that motion as if he'd seen her perform it just yesterday.

"No matter how much we might want to, we can't turn back the clock."

Their gazes caught and held, and he sensed she had questions running through her mind that she wouldn't ask. It was just as well.

"I'm not doing a very good job at giving that tour, now, am I?" Attempting to lighten the mood, he stood away from the fence and pointed, forcing a smile when he felt none. "Over there I'm building a newly fenced area for horses I need to keep close by and monitor. The bulk of the herd will pasture on the quarter section west of the house. And I'm building a couple of shelters out there as well, so they have a place to huddle during bad weather."

"And what about you, Andrew? The house…"

The house was a weird place to be these days. It was full of ghosts, and not all the pleasant kind. It was too quiet, the silence filled only by the harsh words said several years previously. But it had a bed, and a bathroom, and a kitchen, and it was his. He wasn't sure he could ever exorcise the specters of his past from its rooms, but he was going to try. One of these days he'd get up the courage to go through Gerald's things. So far he'd been unable to make it past the doorway of his father's room.

"The house needs some work as well."

"And you want *it* in shape before the benefit too?

He ran a hand through his hair. Lord, there was so much work. Working from dawn to dusk was the only thing getting him to sleep these days; exhaustion was a powerful tool. But for the briefest of moments there were so many items on his to-do list it was overwhelming.

"In a perfect world. But there's so much else to do I can't see how it will happen."

Jen watched as Andrew walked away, over to the porch of the house, putting a hand on the railing leading up the step. He obviously felt very strongly about what he was doing. And he needed help. She was tempted to offer hers. Maybe because he seemed so tired. Maybe because it touched her that he was trying to build something fundamentally good. Maybe it was the fact that the place he needed most seemed to be home, whether he realized it or not. Maybe it was for the simple reason that they'd once been friends, once been lovers. Maybe it was all of those reasons mixed up together.

Her gaze dropped to the back pockets of his jeans as he made his way up the steps; the spit in her mouth pooled as attraction sizzled through her limbs. He'd invited her here to convince her to cater the dance. And it was working. If he asked her at this moment she knew *yes* would come out of her mouth before she could stop it.

"Jen…" He turned, looked down at her and her insides went all woozy.

"What?"

"Why don't you come inside? We can talk more about the dance."

Right. Business. That was exactly where her thoughts should be.

"I don't think that's a good idea." The house held too many memories of their time together. If she were going to do this it was going to be for business reasons, not because of a misplaced sense of nostalgia.

"Why not?"

It was too difficult to come up with plausible reasons without delving too deeply into the truth. Seeing Andrew, being with him, felt much too familiar for her to be comfortable.

"I need to get back. I have some work of my own to do."

He watched her for a few moments, and she felt as though his eyes could see right into her and through the small lie. "I see," he said quietly.

"I'm sorry."

"But you'll cater the party?"

How could she say no? It would be a deliberate snub and she wasn't capable of it. And his enthusiasm had touched her, whether she admitted it to him or not. "Yes, I'll cater," she decided.

He put his hand against the spooled porch railing. "We should talk about the menu, then, and your fee. You sure you don't want to come in for a few minutes?"

Oh, she wanted to. She wanted to spend more time with him, and she was curious about the house now that he was back in it. But she knew it would be a mistake. Especially after the little interlude in the tackroom earlier. She didn't want to be alone with him. Not until the newness of seeing him again had worn off. Right now it was far too fresh.

"Another time? Soon."

"Dinner? Tomorrow night?"

The suggestion came out so quickly she had no time to put up her guard. "Dinner?"

"Come out tomorrow and have dinner. Everyone has to eat."

First of all, unless something had changed over the years, Andrew couldn't cook. And dinner for two out at the secluded ranch was even worse than going inside now. "Why don't you meet me in town?" she suggested. "For pizza. Papa's is still there, you know." In town, in a public restaurant, she'd feel more comfortable. More on her own turf, in control of the situation.

"Papa's it is. I'll pick you up at—"

"I'll meet you there," she broke in quickly. "After all, it's not a date."

"I'll be there at six," he replied, pushing away from the column. He turned and went into the house, the screen door smacking against the frame behind him.

Not a date. Jen worried her lip with her teeth as she walked back to the car. It sure felt like one just the same.

Andrew was waiting for her at Papa's, seated at a table by the front window and scowling into a soft drink. Jen lifted a hand to Jim, the "Papa" behind the name, and exhaled, pasting on a smile. She'd been relieved yesterday to set up their meeting in a public spot, but later had realized the folly of it. She might say it was not a date, but she knew the townspeople of Larch Valley would think that it looked like one.

She sat down across from him. "You're early."

He looked up, a smile breaking out on his face. "I had an errand in town and finished earlier than I expected." As Jen put her purse on the seat, Linda Briggs brought a plastic tumbler and put it on the table. "Andrew ordered you a Dr. Pepper," she said, but Jen detected a bit of steel in the words.

"Thanks, Linda. How's Megan? Last I heard she was down with this spring cold."

"On the mend, thanks for asking," Linda replied.

Jen couldn't help but notice that Linda kept her back half-turned toward Andrew. Had he done something to make her angry? Jen smiled, attempting to lighten the atmosphere that for some reason held a shimmering of tension.

"You kids ready to order?" Linda asked, poising her pen over her small notepad.

Jen looked at Andrew, who was doing a good impression

of being relaxed, leaning back against the vinyl of the booth seat. "You still like everything?"

"Absolutely."

"A medium colossal, then. And could we get a salad to share too?"

"Sure thing, sweetie." Linda scribbled on the pad and went back to the kitchen.

"Wonder what I did to her," Andrew muttered, leaning ahead and picking up his glass. He took a drink and put it down again, moving it in circles on the scratched table top. "She was friendly enough when I came in, but when I asked about your drink she clammed up. You do still like Dr. Pepper, don't you?"

She felt a little uncomfortable, knowing Andrew had deliberately ordered her favorite drink from teenage years. Jen suddenly smiled as realization dawned. She'd known Linda since she'd been a girl. Linda's son Dawson had been friends with both her and Andrew. Linda, in her motherly way, was being protective. The whole town knew Jen had been heartbroken when Andrew had gone away. Her smile faded a bit, as she remembered. She'd been so sure he'd come back. In a town like this, everyone had known she'd been waiting. And they'd known when her heart had been broken too.

Linda was looking out for her, and Jen didn't have it within her to mind. The people of Larch Valley had always been there for her. It was the reason why she'd wanted to stay—even when she'd lost her reason to.

Linda came back with a Caesar salad and two plates, and Jen waited quietly until she went away again. She picked up the plastic tongs and served each of them a helping of the crisp salad.

"You want to know what you did?" Jen asked, picking up the thread of conversation. She looked up at Andrew, who'd irritably picked up his fork. "You didn't come back."

"You're joking. That was years ago." He put down his fork and frowned at her.

"You really have forgotten what Larch Valley is like, then. Memories are long."

"Including yours?"

She felt a little twisting in her stomach at the question. He really had no idea, did he? Maybe it was time he learned. "Especially mine," she replied quietly. "Don't be angry with Linda. She'll come around. I think she always kind of hoped that Dawson and I…"

"You and Dawson?" The question echoed through the eating area and both their heads turned quickly toward the kitchen area before moving back to each other. The gold flecks were sparking in his eyes and she raised her eyebrows.

"Are you jealous?"

He looked away. "Of course not."

Jen picked at her salad. "For the record, no. Not me and Dawson. He's a friend. That's all he's ever been. Linda is just being protective."

"And you obviously need protecting." There was bitterness in the words.

"Hardly. I learned to stand on my own two feet long ago. Anyway, we came to talk about this dance, right?"

She pushed her salad plate aside and pulled out a notebook. "What we're discussing here is business."

"And that's all there is?"

"That's all there can be. Don't you agree?" She felt a certain release in saying the words. "I can't dwell on the past. I moved on, built my own life. Just as you did."

"I know that."

Relief was tempered by a disappointment she didn't want to feel. "I took your job because it makes good business sense. Not out of any feelings of misplaced sentimentality or loyalty."

His throat bobbed as he swallowed and she saw a muscle tick in his jaw. Was he angry at her?

She wrote the word "*Menu*" at the top of a page, but Andrew stopped her with a hand on her arm. She looked up, mesmerized by what she saw in his eyes. Anger, frustration, gratitude…and something more that complicated everything.

"Is that all?"

"It's all there can be, Drew."

Linda chose that particular moment to deliver their pizza, hot and fragrant with tomato and cheese and toppings.

Andrew slid his fingers off of her wrist and looked the waitress square in the face. "Thank you, Mrs. Briggs."

She seemed to soften a little bit. "You're welcome. You kids call if you want something else."

Jen slid a piece of pizza on to her plate, and so did Andrew. "Do you suppose we'll always be considered 'the kids'?" She laughed lightly, trying to dispel the serious atmosphere. The last thing she wanted was for things to get heavy. Why couldn't they leave things behind and be friends? They were both adults.

"We did have some good times, didn't we?"

She took her fork and lifted a black olive off the pizza slice, popping it into her mouth. "Drew…"

"Oh, come on, Jen. How many times did we come here for pizza after a school dance or a movie?" He stared pointedly at her plate. "Do you still eat all the toppings first, and then the crust?"

She couldn't help the grin that crept up her cheek. "Yeah, I guess I do."

"Those were good times."

She would not cry, or sniff, or get sloppily sentimental. She couldn't. "Yes, they were," she replied, fixating on a mushroom buried beneath melted cheese. "Movie theater's closed now, though. And the high school is now the junior high. They built a new high school north of town. Times change."

"People change too, right?"

She gave up on the mushroom. Andrew hadn't even touched his pizza, she realized. He was looking at her as if wanted her to believe him. And she did want to. But she couldn't afford to. It would complicate everything.

But he was right. People did change. "Have you changed? You're back home, so I guess you must have. But I hope you realize that things here didn't necessarily stay the same. Me included."

He frowned, finally picking up his pizza and taking a bite. He swallowed, took his napkin and wiped sauce from his lips. "Oh, I think I've reached that realization," he replied.

Jen realized that several pairs of eyes were watching them now, and she forced a smile. As much as she appreciated the moral support, it had always been a challenge, being under the watchful eye of the town. "One thing that hasn't changed," she said quietly, "Nosy Nellies. I'd say the two of us together is causing a bit of a sensation."

"It's not really a date," he said, but she could see his earlier annoyance was dissipating. "We might as well get down to business and enjoy ourselves. This is way better than anything I could have cooked anyway."

His eyes glowed at her, and she felt a strange sense of accord with him. Perhaps they could move past their old relationship and be friends. Catering his event would be a good start to that.

She slid her plate to the side, took one more bite, and then clicked the top of her pen. "Okay, then. We're thinking finger foods, right? And nothing too fancy."

"Exactly."

"Hot, cold? Do you want dessert?"

"Definitely some sweets. Your brownies, for one. You know, the one thing that didn't surprise me was that you made baking your livelihood, Jen." He slipped another piece of pizza on his plate and smiled at her. "You were always a great baker."

Jen felt a pang of remembrance. She doubted that Andrew realized that his father's death had affected her as well. She could still remember visiting on Saturdays and watching Gerald at the sink, cutting up potatoes and carrots to go with a roast. The house of single men ate plainly, and she'd always brought something for dessert. Cake, or pie, or the banana bread that had been Noah's particular favorite. He'd jokingly said he was going to marry her someday, so she could cook sweets for him all the time. She could very nearly hear their voices, and see Noah's wink at Andrew as he said it, knowing she was Andrew's girl. Andrew had broken her heart, but she'd also felt the loss of her second family acutely.

She'd always promised herself that she'd be rational, sensible, if he came back. But the past had its claws in her and she had to fight to keep the memories from being too bittersweet. She wanted to look back with fondness. If they could just remember the good times, before it had all gone wrong…

"Remember the time Noah decided he was going to make pies? He was back from boot camp and had brought a whole box of fresh apples with him."

Drew laughed now, genuinely entertained. "He absolutely refused your help."

"And the pastry looked like a road crew had come through doing patch work."

"And we all ate it, even though it was tough and the apples were still hard."

"It was better with the ice cream."

They were smiling fully at each other, and when Jen

realized it she dropped her eyes to her plate, stirred more than she cared to admit by the warmth of his gaze.

Andrew saw her gaze drop and his smile faded. She was still so pretty. Fresh and natural, as she had been as a girl, only now with a woman's strength and knowledge. At first he'd missed her so, but then over time it had faded, and he'd convinced himself it was a high school thing. But it wasn't. She still got to him. There *had* been good times before it all blew apart.

"Is it strange, being back in the house, then?"

Her soft voice drew him back from his musings and he sighed. Being in the house again was like looking at a room through a filter. It was a shadow of itself, dusty, faded, stuck in time. He'd walked in and taken stock: the tie-back curtains were limp and faded at the windows, the oak table was scratched and without a tablecloth, the old cushion floor hadn't been scrubbed and waxed in an age. And it was quiet. So very, very quiet.

"The house hasn't really changed," he replied quietly, giving his lips a final wipe with the napkin. "I don't think Dad ever threw anything out. If there was an ounce of use left in it…"

"I know. Even when he went to the care home he took that awful old thirteen-inch TV with him. I tried to convince him to buy a new one, but he said that one was perfectly good. Wouldn't buy a DVD-player either—insisted on watching his old movies on that VCR you bought him for Christmas way back when."

It sounded so typically Gerald that Andrew nearly smiled. But it was that type of obstinacy that had kept them apart. He puckered his brow, wondering why Jen couldn't see that. "You spent a lot of time with him?"

"Not so much. A visit here and there. He was lonely. He missed you."

Andrew's lips pursed as he watched her reach up to tuck a stubborn piece of hair behind her ear.

"Would you like me to tell you about him? Maybe it would help."

He crumpled up the napkin and tossed it on the table. Having to hear about Gerald from Jen was like taking a stinging cut and then poring salt on it. "Help with what, exactly?"

Her eyes widened. "You must miss him."

He laughed soundlessly, little humor in his expression. "Yeah."

"He missed you too. He made sure that Elsie at the library kept tabs on…"

"Let's get one thing straight, shall we?" He lowered his voice, trying to keep the shake out of it, trying to keep the people at the nearby tables from hearing. Lord, he'd spent years trying to get his father's attention—to no avail. What did Jen possibly know about that? About how hard he'd worked to prove himself to the old man, to show that he'd made the right choice by following his own dreams? "I appreciate the sentiment, really I do. But talking about Gerald is a no-go zone."

"But…"

"I mean it, Jen."

"Can I ask why?"

He stood up, reaching inside his pocket for a few bills which he tossed on the table. "I don't know what you think you know, but Gerald Laramie didn't give a damn about what I did once I left Lazy L."

Without waiting to hear her response, he strode to the door and swung it open, walking out into the spring evening.

CHAPTER FOUR

JEN hastily grabbed her purse and notebook. Her heart ached as realization struck. Was he so hurt by his father's death then that even talking about it was simply too much? She thought back to when they'd met after the funeral. He'd been alone. Noah had been deployed and hadn't made it back. She'd offered her condolences but he'd brushed by her as if she were nothing. But maybe he'd been too full of grief. Maybe it hadn't been about her at all.

She followed him out the door, taking quick strides to catch him as he made his way up the avenue toward the park. "Drew, wait," she called softly. His steps slowed but they did not stop. And she began to wonder if Andrew's sudden appearance at Lazy L, his sudden change of heart, hadn't been prompted by his father in the first place. She owed it to Gerald to tell Andrew some of the things his father had said during the last years. But not today. It would fall on deaf ears.

She caught up with him at the park, where he'd dropped onto a bench, staring out at the trees that were just starting to bud. The sound of laughter and the creak of swings came from the playground. She didn't know what to say to him now, so merely sat down beside him, considering the odd turn of events that had taken her life and turned it upside down over the past few months. Here she was, taking the biggest business risk she could remember, and sharing breathing space with Andrew Laramie on a spring evening. It was a stark reminder that she had her life now and he had his, and they weren't joined in any way. And yet it was so clear to her that he was hurting. How could she turn him away when what she really wanted was to help him?

"Today was a bit of a trip down memory lane, wasn't it?" She crossed her left leg over her right, all her senses tuned to his every move. His shoulders lifted up and down as he sighed. She marveled at how he could be as familiar to her as the scent of a summer rain kissing a dusty road and yet be a total stranger. Once upon a time she would have been able to read his thoughts.

"Perhaps."

She fought back the urge to sigh and tried an encouraging smile instead. "Maybe it would have been better if we'd just stuck to menus."

She wished he'd look at her, so she could see the answer in his eyes. But he just stared resolutely out over the grass. His shoulders tensed slightly and she knew she'd struck a nerve.

"Undoubtedly."

"You know, I was mad at you for a long time, Drew."

"I know."

"But only because I was hurt."

She saw him flinch as her words struck home.

"I just want to be honest. We're not eighteen anymore. And while I've agreed to help you because of business..."

"We both know this is more than business."

His words were like lighting a match to kindling, the fire catching and burning. "I can't dwell on the past. I moved on, built my own life. Just as you did."

"I know that."

His throat bobbed as he swallowed, and she saw him clench

his jaw. Was he angry at her? She almost smiled. It would be one of the first true indications that he had any feelings on the matter at all.

"But there's more to it, isn't there? Let me be your friend, Drew."

He turned his head, and for a few moments he seemed to be the man she remembered. "It was good, talking about some of the memories," he said quietly. "I know I hired you, but it was good having dinner with a friend."

What could she say to that? She couldn't read his eyes; he'd dropped the shutters on them again. She wasn't sure they could actually *be* friends. Too much water under the bridge and all that. And yet to be more was unthinkable. He had already broken her heart once.

"Either way you slice it, you've got this benefit to think of first. We can talk about Gerald another time."

"Or not."

So cold. So cut off. She worried her hands together as she wondered about his determination to avoid anything to do with his father. Maybe all he needed was time. He hadn't been home long, after all.

"We didn't even do any menu-planning. Why don't I work up a preliminary list? That way you can veto anything that doesn't suit and we can come up with some alternatives."

"That would be good."

"Right." She got up, tucking the notebook back in her bag. "Thanks for dinner."

He rose too, and took a step toward her. "I'm sorry it ended the way it did."

She wanted to ask why, but knew she'd be faced with his stony silence again. She understood that whatever it was, he wasn't ready to talk about it. But the moment drew out, as if he was waiting for her to say something. And all the time she was trying not to look at his lips, or to remember the way they felt and tasted, or the way he'd always been pulling her pony-tail elastic out to run his fingers through her hair. Her toes nearly curled just thinking about it.

"We'll talk soon." She offered a polite smile, though her heart was thumping. She spun and hurried off back down the street toward her car.

She got in, slamming the door. Friends, indeed. If that were true, why did she very nearly feel his kiss on her lips?

And why did she want it so badly?

Jen wasn't at all certain that the color she'd chosen for the interior—chocolate cherry—was the right one.

Paint smeared an old white T-shirt and dotted the tip of her nose as she peered up at the line where the white ceiling and the reddish-rose wall met.

The bakery kitchen was still a shambles as the contractors restructured and rewired for additional equipment, and the flooring for the café section wouldn't arrive until next week, but Jen was bound and determined that the walls be painted, so that once the flooring was installed the trim and crown molding could follow right away.

But she was getting tired. She was working double duty pre-paring for the benefit at Lazy L as well as at Snickerdoodles, and she would be glad when Sunday rolled around and the dance was over. She'd have her check and could make her first payment on her loan before she even reopened.

She sighed, retied the bandana over her hair, poured paint into the plastic tray and picked up her roller.

She was halfway through the first wall when knocking came from the front door. "We're closed!" she called out, but seconds later the knocking came louder. With a sigh she put down her roller and went to the door.

"I'm sorry, the bakery is—"

"Closed. Yeah, I know."

Drew, standing there in the shadows as the streetlights just started to flicker on. His grin was lopsided and boyish, and she lowered her lashes before he could see how happy she was to see him. She shouldn't be. She'd drawn a line in the sand that meant *strictly business*. Or at least *strictly friends*. She wasn't planning on crossing it. Heck, she'd even decided another meeting was not a good idea and had e-mailed him a tentative menu instead of seeing him face to face. All she'd been able to think about was the way he'd looked at her as they'd sat in the park.

She'd made some samples and delivered them when she was sure he'd be out of the house. And now here he was—live, breathing, and in her construction zone.

He stepped inside and looked around at the chaos. Jen had a moment of female vanity where she realized she was in her worst clothes, with an old bandana tied over her hair and paint smudges on everything. It quickly passed…she was simply a business owner working hard to stay afloat. She was proud of what she was doing. And certainly not too proud to do her share of the work. It shouldn't matter what she looked like.

"Did you need something in particular?"

The words came out slightly snappish. She was annoyed at herself for caring about her appearance. His booted feet left footprints in the fine film of drywall dust still sifting about on the floors as he walked the perimeter, casually examining it.

"I came to say thank you, actually."

Jen tried to ignore the persistent ache in her shoulders—the one put there from spending the day painting. When John, her painter, had called and explained that his young daughter had been in an accident and would be in the hospital for a few days, she'd never given it a second thought. The last thing she wanted him to worry about was work. And rather than fall behind she'd picked up a brush and roller and had started the café walls herself. The more she could pitch in, the faster it would all go.

The distraction of Andrew wasn't helping her accomplish that goal.

"Say thank you for what?" She had to stop standing there like a lovestruck idiot. Pasting a neutral expression on her face, she went back to her stepladder and paint tray, rolling an even coat on the sponge and stepping up to roll the top part of the wall.

"For dropping over all those samples this week." He followed her, stopping at the base of the ladder and tilting his chin up. She tried valiantly to ignore him. Tonight he wore a khaki colored T-shirt that should have been boringly neutral but instead brought out the greeny-gold of his eyes, so that one color nearly reflected the other. She made a point *not* to gaze into them.

"Did you make a final decision?" There weren't that many days left, and she needed to get shopping and cooking for the final menu. And perhaps manage a few hours of sleep at some point.

"I did." He patted his jeans pocket and her eyes were diverted to the worn denim. "Right here. I have to admit, your goodies pulled double duty."

"How so?" She bit down on her lip, intent on focusing on the wall.

"They kept me from having to cook a couple of times. And tasted better than boxed macaroni and cheese. Other than the pizza we shared, meals have been a bit sketchy out at the house."

So he didn't cook much for himself. She wasn't sure if she was pleased he seemed to have a weakness or annoyed with the fact that perhaps he'd never needed to learn.

She refilled her roller and rubbed it on the wall in front of her. "If you want to leave your final choices on the ledge over there, I'll get them when I'm done," she said, weariness leaking through her tone.

"Done?" He took a step closer to the ladder. "You can't mean to do all this tonight. It's after nine o'clock."

"I need to get this coat on so it will be dry for the next one tomorrow. Even with the tinted primer it's going to take three coats."

"I thought you'd hired contractors."

"I did."

"Then why aren't they doing it?"

She inched over on the ladder, reaching for a spot on her right that she'd missed. "They are. I'm helping. The less time I'm closed, the better."

"Is money that tight, then?" he said quietly.

Every ounce of pride in her bristled. The roller ran faster and faster over the wall. "I'm just a small business owner, trying to keep up during a challenging financial climate." She smiled grimly, absurdly proud of herself for that sentence. "But that's not why, if you must know. I hired John Barker to paint for me, but his youngest is in hospital and he needed a few days off."

"Is it serious?"

Her shoulders relaxed slightly at the genuine concern she heard in his voice. They'd both gone to school with John since first grade. "I don't think so. But the last thing he needs to worry about is the job, you know? He'll be back next week."

"No one could ever accuse you of being lazy, Jen."

"Thank you."

"They might accuse you of being a bit of a bleeding heart, though."

Bleeding heart? When it was simply a matter of neighbor

helping neighbor? "Maybe you haven't spent much time in places where people help each other, Andrew. Where they look out for each other."

"A person doesn't like to assume he's welcome in a place. Maybe a fella likes to be asked."

She scowled. It was bad enough she'd taken his catering job to begin with; bad enough she had to see him as often as she did. And definitely awful to realize that she was just as attracted to him now as she'd been then. Maybe even more so. It was difficult to keep her mind on business when her thoughts kept leading her elsewhere.

"Maybe if a fella *offered* his help once in a while, he'd feel a lot more welcome," she retorted.

"All right." His voice was deep and oddly quiet again—the way it got when it could reach right inside her and turn things upside down. "Would you like my help, Jen?"

She swallowed. Yes, definitely. The gently worded question did soften her toward him considerably—even if she had been the one to practically script it for him and give him a nudge. Was she really so weak when it came to him? She hoped not.

"I'm fine. Really and truly." She lowered her chin and pinned him with what she hoped was a stern look. "I'm *always* fine."

"Yes. I know." He conceded her point softly, and she forgot her goal to avoid his eyes. Now his were soft and mossy-colored with understanding, fringed with his stupidly long lashes. Her tummy flipped over as the moment drew out. She did not want his understanding or his pity. He couldn't know, after all. He hadn't been here to see the damage he'd done. She'd be a fool to let him in again, wouldn't she?

"I did come to ask a small favor." He finally said something, though his eyes never left her face and her own were drawn down to stare at his full lips as he spoke. "Something special for the benefit."

"Something special?" She'd already pored over her recipe books trying to find the kind of foods his guests were likely to enjoy. Plain, substantial food, yet with a festive, elegant twist. It had been more difficult than she'd expected. Now, as she watched his lips move, she realized he was too close. She inched farther over on the step.

"A recipe." He looked as if he was about to choke on the words. "I thought maybe it would be a good addition."

She stared at him. "My menu wasn't complete, I take it?"

"No! Of course not. I mean, it was fine," he amended. "I just came across this the other night when I was going through the kitchen. I thought if anybody could make sense of it, you could."

He reached into his pocket and withdrew a small slip of paper, handing it over. "It was one of Gerald's favorites."

The confession was made so softly she knew it had been difficult for him to say. After his quick refusal to even speak his father's name at dinner, she knew it was a big thing for him to reach out even this much. She took the paper, scanning the faded handwriting.

"This is it?" There was hardly anything on it, just rudimentary ingredients, no measurements, no method.

"I know it's rough…but you're such a good cook, Jen. I felt certain when I saw it that you could adapt it for the function." He looked up at her, his eyes warm with confidence. "I haven't had it since I was a small boy. Mum used to make it for Gerald's birthday."

Andrew kept referring to his father as Gerald, and she wondered if it was part of the way he was handling his grief. The little bit of distance to make it easier. She wanted to ask, but he'd made it clear he didn't want to talk about it. She didn't want to start another argument.

And, as much as she wanted to help, there was the added

work to consider. She'd have to experiment first—see if she could get it right.

"I don't know, Drew. It's not very complete, and I'd have to experiment a bit. And even if I did make it, it might not taste like you remember." A sudden thought struck her. Many of the selections she'd picked were make-ahead, with the consideration that she was without much of her bakery equipment. The old oven was gone and the new one ordered and not yet delivered. She was down to the stove in her house. If she adapted this recipe, it had to be with a mind toward her limited capabilities.

"I'm sure it'll be great," he murmured, fueling her doubts. He took one more imploring step forward, his booted toe bumping the stepladder as Jen tried backing up and found nowhere to go.

His boot hit one leg of the ladder and her weight was mostly over on the other. She watched as the paint started to slop in the tray hanging on the front of the ladder and lurched forward to steady it. She did, but then the center of gravity of the ladder shifted, throwing her off-balance once more. Her foot reached for the step that was no longer there.

She knew she was falling and powerless to stop it. There was a sense of weightlessness as gravity took over and nothing was beneath her feet. She braced herself for a big bump on the hard, concrete floor. Only it never came.

Instead she was caught by two strong arms, one unceremoniously hooked beneath her left armpit, the other tangled up between their bodies as he bolstered her weight. She twisted, opening her mouth to rail at him for causing the accident, then her gaze caught his and the words vaporized before reaching her lips.

Other than the once he'd touched her waist in passing, they'd avoided physical contact. Even in the tackroom it had been the one barrier not crossed. But now...now she was held in his arms, unable to avoid the strength there, or the hard, warm feel of his length against her in several places along her body. In his arms. The one place she'd never thought she'd be ever again. It was both sad and electric.

And, by the flare in his eyes, she wasn't the only one feeling the current.

His hot gaze dropped to her lips, and she felt them open slightly as her breath accelerated with acknowledgment. *He's going to kiss me*, she realized, while in her brain denial fought to be heard. It wasn't loud enough. For the briefest of seconds their lips hovered, only an inch apart. And then he tightened the arm around her ribs and his mouth was on hers.

Her heart slammed into her ribs, pounding against the biceps that held her so tightly against his body so hard that she was sure he must be able to feel it through his skin. His lips were warm and soft, yet controlling, demanding she return in kind. It was a demand she couldn't help but answer as her mouth opened beneath his.

The moment she acquiesced the world tilted sideways. Andrew turned slightly, unpinning his trapped arm and wrapping it around the top of her shoulders. His fingers gripped her neck beneath the hair cascading from her bandana. He shifted, planting his feet on the concrete, a solid place for her body to curve into as she melted against him.

His hand left her neck briefly to pull the bandana off her head, and she felt his fingers twine in her hair. And, oh, he tasted the same as she remembered. She shouldn't be able to recall the flavor that was simply *Drew*, but one touch of his lips on hers and it came flooding back with disturbing clarity.

Finally he broke the kiss, resting his lips against her temple with a sigh. Their breathing echoed through the empty space.

"Jen," he whispered, and her eyes closed as the sound of

her name on his lips reached inside of her and held on. It was as good as she remembered. It was better.

His hand lay against her head, almost as if he was tracing the shape of it with his palm, and she leaned into the contact. The taste, the smell of him, the feel of his body against hers— those senses all lent themselves to a strange feeling of security, as if she'd never left.

And then she remembered. *She* wasn't the one who'd done the leaving. He had.

She pulled away out of his arms, stumbling backward past the ladder and the drop cloth. How could she have fallen under his spell so quickly? After she'd promised herself she wouldn't? After making her wishes perfectly clear that evening at the park? Platonic only! She ran her tongue over her lips, trying to wash the taste of him away and failing utterly.

"Jen," he cautioned, and the indulgent tone of his voice did absolutely nothing to comfort her.

"Was this your sales pitch, Drew?" She wished the words had come out strong and defiant rather than with a tell-tale wobble. In her consternation she'd forgotten she didn't want to call him Drew, and that aggravated her further. She forced herself to calm. "Did you think kissing me would convince me to help you? To take on more work?"

"That's not why I kissed you!" He took a step forward, eyes flashing, and she could feel the memory of his wide chest against hers only moments before. Her fingers itched to touch it again, to see if it really felt as strong as it had seemed.

"Then why did you?"

A hush fell over the room. Suddenly Jen didn't want to know the answer. The possibilities were far too frightening when she'd spent so much energy first getting over him and then building her own life without him.

"Because I had to know."

She swallowed. Fear fought with undeniable curiosity. "Had to know what?"

Was there really several feet between them? It didn't feel as if there was. Lord, even from this distance it felt like he was touching her, and she couldn't escape it. It was as if the space she'd attempted to put between them didn't even exist.

"If you tasted the same."

Every dying hope she'd had was suddenly resurrected and swelled into her chest. She tried beating it down. This wasn't what she wanted. She refused to fall under his spell again, knowing that in all likelihood it would end when he'd had his fill of home and went to seek his fortunes again. And yet her own reaction demanded she know the truth about his.

"And did I?" She lifted her chin.

And finally, finally, he broke eye contact. "Yes," he admitted, and she could clearly see that the result didn't make him as happy as it apparently had when they had been engaged in the actual activity.

"You left me," she whispered, shattered. "I haven't forgotten."

"Neither have I."

She supposed it was as much of an admission of guilt as she'd get out of him. It wasn't his fault she couldn't seem to shake her feelings for him. Clearly they'd never gone away but had only been put in storage, waiting for his return to be brought out and dusted off. Feelings were one thing. But letting him see them was quite another. And they'd both admitted there was no going back.

"I agreed to cater your dance for two reasons," she said, desperately trying to regain her emotional footing. "One being it's good for *my* business. Secondly, I think what you're doing is a good thing, and it's something I am proud to be a part of."

"Jen, I—"

"I'm not finished." She drew on all her inner strength.

"This does not mean I'm interested in starting anything up with you. I'm certainly not a convenience you can use when you need something done."

He stepped forward and she knew she'd hit a nerve by the sharp angle of his jaw and the way his lips thinned.

"You have never been a convenience," he gritted out. He turned away, paced a few feet, and his shoulders rose and fell even though she didn't hear the sigh. He hooked his thumbs in his pockets before turning back, and some of the heat and panic drained out of her.

"You're insulted," he said. "You're insulted, and that was not my intention at all. When I thought of it, it was because of two things and two things only. One, you're the best cook I know, and if anyone has a hope of recreating this it's you. I'm certainly not Martha Stewart enough to try it."

She tried hard to keep her lips from twitching; the very thought of Andrew being anything like the domestic icon was laughable.

"And the second reason was that I'm coming to realize you were close to my father. Maybe closer than I ever was. I thought you might like to do it."

"Why? Because I'm a soft touch?"

He shook his head. "No, Jen. Because you're you."

It shouldn't have touched her, but it did. He understood. Perhaps he even understood that she could never willingly turn her back on someone in need—even him.

This was the first time he'd mentioned anything about wanting to connect with memories of his father, and even though a tiny voice inside her warned her it was a bad idea, she wanted to help him with that.

"Why is this so important to you? It's just one dish."

Andrew took his time replying, first walking over to the counter that had held the cash register not that long ago. Now it was covered with a cloth, and he ran his finger over it, leaving a trail and getting drywall dust on his fingertip.

"Lazy L is my home, Jen. But I can't live in the past anymore. I need to move forward. I just want to live in the present. To start over. And to do that I realize I can't keep ignoring my past. I need to accept it."

Boy, could she relate to that. It was a good reason, and one that made sense.

The welcoming feel at Lazy L had come from Gerald and Noah and Andrew. Now there was just Andrew, and who would welcome him? He was asking for her help, and she suddenly realized how difficult that must have been. The Andrew she remembered didn't like to ask anyone for anything. His kiss still tingled on her lips.

"If I do this, I expect to be reimbursed for everything I buy." She forced herself to keep the terms businesslike, so he wouldn't see how much his plea touched her.

"Naturally."

"And don't expect a miracle. I'm in the middle of renovations here, and already cooking for Saturday night."

"Of course not."

She had to be insane, the way she kept agreeing to do things for him.

"And you'll have to be available to taste test. I can't possibly make something to taste like you remember if I don't know what that is." Belatedly she realized she'd just come up with an additional reason to see him. She couldn't seem to keep her distance from him even when she tried!

"Whatever you say."

Hah, she thought, *it's whatever* you *say when you're getting your way.* And yet she remembered Gerald saying to her, not long before he died, to go easy on Andrew when he came back. As if he'd known his son would return when Jen had known no such thing. She felt she should do this, just knowing it was one of Gerald's favorites from years ago.

"Then you have a deal." She turned away from him and went back to the ladder, heart pounding. "Now, get going so I can finish this up before midnight."

"Thank you, Jen. Again."

The sincerity in his voice touched her, and she closed her eyes briefly, knowing he was looking at her back.

"Don't thank me yet," she advised, picking up the roller and filling it with paint once more. "I might mess this up completely."

He came forward, put his hands on her shoulders, and placed a kiss on her forehead. The spot burned where his lips had been.

"Thank you anyway," he murmured, as she closed her eyes. His footsteps went away, and then she heard the shutting of the door. Only after he was gone did she put the roller down and hang her head, admitting to herself that he still had the power to put her heart in tatters.

CHAPTER FIVE

JEN decided to use Andrew's house to experiment with the recipe, since her bungalow was home to many of the supplies from the bakery. There was barely enough space for her to put together a meal for herself, let alone try anything extra. On the night of the benefit she'd be using his kitchen anyway. She could use the time to get a feel for working in his space.

With only a few days left until the dance, she could also start taking some of what she needed out there, saving her trips on Friday and Saturday. No doubt Andrew thought it was a matter of throwing together a little bit of food, but she knew it was much, much more involved than that.

But the last coat of paint hadn't gone on until after four o'clock, so it was nearly dinnertime when she finally finished packing the car and headed west to Lazy L.

She noticed the difference in the property the moment she turned up the drive. The fences leading to the house and surrounding the corral had been repaired and painted a blinding white. Someone had made a first cut of the grass around the house, and the pale green spears bore the newness of spring growth. It no longer looked neglected. It looked like it had a purpose.

The front door was unlocked when she took the crock pot

of roast inside. She put the pot down on the table. Whatever the improvements outside, they hadn't been extended to in here. It was bland, faceless, without a single stamp of personality and in dire need of updating. It was a house, she realized, but not a home. Andrew could say all he wanted about moving on. The old house was exactly as it had been left. She wondered why he hadn't seen fit to add his own belongings rather than keeping old remnants of his childhood. A shrine to happier times?

Shrugging, she went back outside. It wasn't her place to decide how Andrew did or didn't decorate his house. Her only immediate concern was Saturday night's success. She went back to the car and took out her supplies; the flatware and dishes she'd ordered for her catering business hadn't arrived yet, so she'd decided to make do with paper plates and napkins made from recycled paper. Thank goodness the chafing dishes had been delivered, and the platters. There'd be no need to worry about keeping the hot dishes hot and the cold, cold.

She was on her last few bags when Andrew came around the corner from the barn and she stopped, her heart skipping a beat.

He'd obviously spent the afternoon at some sort of manual labor. His boots were dusty and streaks of dirt ran up his jeans. His T-shirt was crumpled and carried the same film of dust as his boots. A brown Stetson was pulled low over his eyes, shading out the afternoon sun.

He looked hot, and dirty, and undeniably sexy.

Jen raised her head and stiffened her spine. It was bad enough she'd melted in his arms the other night. It wouldn't do to let it happen again. She wasn't the kind to turn her back on a friend, and it was obvious he was still struggling to come to terms with Gerald's death. There were just limits, that was all.

"I brought some things out. I hope that's okay." She called

over to him, turning away so he wouldn't see the flush in her cheeks or the way her tongue wet her lips.

She'd help him get his feet beneath him. Be neighborly. Once the benefit was over he'd be reconnected with lots of Larch Valley people. He needed to make that connection. She knew that Linda Briggs wasn't the only one in town who had a long memory. It wasn't just her that he'd left. It was all of them. If he wanted the rescue ranch to be a success, he had to win the town over as well. And if she could forgive him for leaving, surely they could as well.

"That's fine," he called back, his voice low and gravelly. "Sorry I wasn't here to let you in."

He sidled across the yard and she exhaled, trying to will away the increase in her heart rate caused by nothing more than his proximity.

"The door was unlocked."

"Right. I forgot. Old habits." He smiled, the corner of his mouth quirking up the way it always did when he flirted. What other old habits could he be thinking of?

She walked ahead of him, taking the bags to the door. He held open the screen while she went in. People didn't tend to lock their doors around here, but she supposed they did where he'd been living.

She put the bags on the table. "I brought out the things to make your beef mixture," she explained. Cooking, at least, was one activity she could do where she felt very much in control. She looked up and smiled. "The beef is cooked. I'm going to pull it and mix up the sauce. Then it'll be your turn, once it has simmered."

Andrew looked down at his jeans and back up, a crooked smile creasing his lips at the volume of dirt marring the blue fabric. "Mind if I shower first?"

She swallowed. The innocent question was suddenly filled

with innuendo, and she wasn't prepared for the heat that rushed through her body at the thought of his muscled limbs under the shower spray.

"Go ahead. This will be a while." She could do this without looking foolish. She adopted a bland expression. "Take your time."

He pulled off his boots and left them by the door, walking down the hall to the stairs that led to the second floor. She snuck a look at his rear view as he went. Lord-a-mercy, the worn denim looked as if it had been made just for him—complete with a streak of dirt right across his backside.

As he turned to go up the stairs she snapped her head back to the pot that held the roast, moving it to a countertop and plugging it in. She opened a drawer, finding two forks in exactly the same place they'd been over a decade earlier. Another drawer held a scarred old cutting board. She put the roast on it and covered it to keep it warm while she mixed the sauce mixture with the small amount of drippings in the ceramic pot. As she whisked it all together she took out a small bottle and measured out three tablespoons of brown liquid, adding it to the mixture.

As the shower started running upstairs, she took the two forks and pulled the beef apart, shredding it into small pieces. She added the tender meat to the sauce, the spicy tomato scent meeting her nose.

The shower stopped and she imagined Drew reaching for a towel…

Several seconds later she realized her hands had paused over her task and she shook her head, chiding herself. It wouldn't do to start thinking about him that way. A dry laugh escaped her lips. Start? She'd done nothing *but* think about him since that day on the street.

She took out a small container of mini brioche buns and sliced them in half, just to keep her hands busy.

She was getting out two plates when his steps sounded on the stairs. She stirred the beef that was soaking up the barbecue sauce, keeping her back to him as he entered the room.

"It smells good in here."

"Did you want to try the sauce? I can still tweak it."

She put the lid down on the countertop and held up a teaspoon. The rich smell wafted into the air, and her stomach rumbled. She'd hardly had time for lunch today, between painting and packing things up for Lazy L. And now, with food so nearly ready, her stomach was announcing its hunger.

Andrew took the teaspoon and stepped up to the pot, dipping it in and tasting the sauce.

He closed his eyes and she watched his throat bob as he swallowed, watched as he licked a remnant of sauce off his top lip.

"Well?"

"It's good. It's really close, Jen. Maybe…a little more something. A little more heat."

She took out a small bottle and added a few drops, stirring it around. "You won't be able to tell the true difference right away. It has to simmer in it."

But she could tell by his smile that she'd managed to decipher the recipe well enough. She picked up a mini-bun and spooned a small amount of beef onto it, covering it with the rounded top. "Try this. I tried baking these this morning to make them appetizer-sized. What do you think?"

He finished the bun in two bites, chewing and swallowing in a way that kept Jen's eyes glued to his face.

"That's delicious. I think…" His voice faded away and his throat bobbed once more. His eyes lost their impish gleam and Jen was at a loss to know why the sudden change had come over him.

"What is it? Is there something wrong with it? Too much Worcestershire?"

"No, nothing like that." He reached over for a paper towel and ripped a strip off the roll, wiping his hands. "I was just going to say I think even Mum would approve."

Andrew never talked about his mother. It had always been simply understood. Jen remembered her parents reading her the riot act one day when she'd come home from second grade, talking about how Andrew Laramie didn't have a mom. They'd made it clear that it wasn't acceptable to tease or taunt him about it in any way, shape or form. She'd felt sorry for Andrew then, and years later, when they'd started dating, he'd said very plainly that his mother had left them when he was five. Not since then had he ever mentioned her.

"How much do you remember?" she asked softly, hoping to keep the conversation going. *Casual, easy*, she cautioned herself.

"Not much," he admitted. "I remember her making this for my dad. I remember them laughing. And I remember them fighting." Defiantly he switched on the tap and got a glass of water, but then held it, forgotten, in one hand. "I remember coming home and realizing she was gone."

It was more than he'd ever admitted to her before, and her heart ached at the obvious pain he still felt about it. "I'm sorry, Drew," she murmured, putting her hand on his arm. "That must have been very tough for a little boy."

Andrew seemed to remember where he was, and snapped out of whatever reverie he'd gone into. He lifted the glass and took a long drink. "It doesn't matter now. We're all grown up, and I've got this place and my own life. I'm sorry I brought it up."

I'm not, she realized. What she didn't understand was, if he carried around so much hurt about his mother, what had possessed him to literally ignore the one parent who'd been determined to see him through? She longed to ask him. But she got the feeling she'd be faced with that stony brick wall again.

Without meeting her gaze, he reached out for another bun.

"I didn't mean to make you uncomfortable. I'm usually not sentimental."

"You didn't. Of course you have memories here. This is your home." She reached for another bag on the table. "You don't have to nibble on those. You'll be all night filling up. Here."

She took out two Kaiser buns and put them on plates. "If you don't mind me joining you, I haven't had dinner yet either."

He cleared a space at the table while she heaped the buns with barbecue beef. She handed him a plate and took out one more container—a bowl with a snap lid. She took the cover off and made impromptu salad forks out of two soup spoons.

"What's this?"

"Spinach and cranberry salad."

Andrew sat at his seat, wondering what to do about the quandary he was now in. He was having a meal with Jen O'Keefe. Only she wasn't just Jen O'Keefe. She was Larch Valley's darling. He'd seen that clearly enough the other night at Papa's. She was the girl he'd lost his virginity with. And she was the girl he'd left behind without a word of explanation. How much more complicated could a guy get? He couldn't stop thinking about her, about how he'd kissed her at the bakery when he had known all along he would have to go slowly, gently. Complicated.

"Aren't you going to eat?"

He marveled at how she could sit there as if this was something that happened any day of the week when his insides were twisting with nerves. It had nothing to do with the Tabasco in the sauce or the poppy seed dressing on the salad.

He'd made peace with so much over the last months. He'd been so confident he could come back here and start over. But he'd been wrong. This didn't feel like home. He felt like a stranger here. Jen was the one person who made anything seem familiar, comfortable. As if he belonged. And yet…he couldn't explain to her all the reasons. Not when he still didn't understand them himself.

"Aren't you hungry?"

She paused and looked up at him, her smoky blue eyes wide and questioning. She had no idea of the battle within him, of how he'd simply found himself worn out with it all and was seeking some peace. Maybe even a chance to put some ghosts to rest.

He forced a smile, not wanting to burden her with his troubles. "Just thinking about all there is to do before Saturday night."

"I've been thinking about that. Snickerdoodles is having its electrical done tomorrow, and I'm not going to get my deliveries until next week. John's daughter is out of the hospital, and he's putting up my crown molding in the main room tomorrow. I'm basically off the hook for a few days. I can help."

The offer was at once a godsend and a nightmare. An extra set of hands would be mighty welcome. But the fact that they were Jen's hands threw a kink in the works. He wanted her around. He craved her company. She was like a ray of sunshine wherever she went. But it was harder and harder for him to think of making amends when he kept thinking about kissing her, thinking about the way her hair smelled or her skin felt beneath his fingers...

Definitely complicated.

"You don't have to..."

"Isn't that what you're paying me for? What's left to do?"

"I'm building the band stage in the morning. I've got to make a run into town for the drink supplies. And...oh, dammit, I forgot about coolers." He ran a hand through his hair. "I haven't even thought about decoration. Do I need it for a barn dance?"

She shook her head and laughed. "You didn't ask Lucy for help, did you?"

"No. She offered initially, but I figured she had her hands full with Brody and with the baby coming."

"The baby's not here yet, and Brody's probably driving her crazy. I'll make a call. There's always washtubs out there you can put the beer in. What about lights?"

"Lights?"

"Twinkle lights. You got any?"

Lord, she was talking about twinkle lights? He was setting up a practice, getting in feed for the horses that would be arriving. "I had the fences painted…"

She made a sound in her throat that he didn't like at all. He'd had priorities other than *twinkle lights*.

"Straw bales?" She leaned over her plate and looked deep into his eyes. The way she blinked—the long lashes kissing her cheeks before lifting back up—could make a man lose his train of thought completely.

"Straw bales? Yeah, I've got some of those for bedding…"

She leaned back in her chair, laughing lightly. "Gee, Andrew, you don't need a caterer, you need an event-planner."

"Lucy looked after inviting the businesses and the ranchers and the media."

Jen shook her head and pushed her plate away. "You can't have them all coming here like this. A mowed lawn and some white paint doesn't make a party." She got up and went to her purse, pulling out her notepad and making a list.

"What are you doing?"

"Putting together a barn dance."

"Jen, I really don't—"

"Is there going to be anyone coming in here? In the house?"

"Probably. The bathroom's in here."

"Well, we can't have it looking like this," she remarked.

"It's still stuck in the eighties." She jotted down something else, and his blood pressure went up another ten points. When had he suddenly lost control of the situation?

"Stop. Stop making your list."

She looked up, a mask of confusion marring her face and making a tiny, adorable wrinkle just above her nose.

"What's wrong?"

She folded her hands over her tablet and looked up.

Damn it all, now she'd gone and made him feel stupid. Like when he'd used to get mad at school and the teacher had worn that same *Let's just wait until you calm down* indulgent look. He took two breaths. "You're already doing enough."

"Andrew," she began, her voice steady but soft, "you need help. I'm offering it. It's as simple as that."

"It's too much." He knew she would think he meant too much for her, but he meant too much for him. Already he was feeling the lure of her, the soft sweetness of her generosity weaving its spell like it had all those years ago. She'd weave her way right in here if he wasn't careful. He'd find himself telling her things. Things he'd kept to himself for a long time. Things he was afraid for her to know.

"I don't plan on doing it by myself. I'm very good at delegating," she smiled. His unease multiplied exponentially. The last thing he wanted was for this to be a whole community production, especially when the welcome wagon hadn't been all that warm.

And yet…he did want Lazy L Rescue Ranch to be a community-type project. Not something he hid away and did, but something he could build and be proud of. Something Gerald would have been proud of. This was the launch. And she was right. He wasn't prepared for a party and it was rushing toward him like a freight train.

He looked around the kitchen with its many supplies.

Already there were tables from the church sitting folded in his barn, waiting to be set up.

"Who else is going to do it?"

He scowled, hating that she was right. He needed her. There was no two ways about it.

"If you do come out…"

"Carry on with what you're doing. You won't even know I'm here." She sat back with a satisfied smile.

But *he* would know. And he'd get used to her being around. Worse, he'd miss her when she was gone. And she surely would be gone once she knew the real truth about why he'd left Larch Valley.

Andrew saw changes in the barn and the farmhouse, even though he'd seen little of Jen. He'd heard her car drive up after lunch, but he'd been so busy that he hadn't even gone up to offer her a greeting.

But coming inside now, the night before the dance, he could see she'd come and gone.

Her touches were everywhere.

The kitchen had changed drastically since Jen's appearance. The drab, limp curtains were gone, replaced by pristine white ones with pale yellow daisies dancing around the hem. A bit more feminine than he would have chosen, but they made the room look homier than he ever remembered it being. A yellow and white checked cloth covered the scratched table, and a chrome holder held white paper napkins in the middle. A new microwave graced a corner of the counter—Gerald had never conceded to the need of one—and there were matching white and yellow dishcloths and drying towels hanging over the old towel bar to the left of the sink. It was as if she'd let in a ray of sunshine to the drab old room.

There was a note leaned up against the coffee maker, and

he ignored the welcoming beat of his heart at the sight of it. He should never have kissed her at the bakery. Or encouraged her with puppy-dog looks. She'd woven her spell and had him all wrapped up with a bow at the end of it. He had to be careful not to get caught simply because it was easy being with her. Jen wasn't the kind of woman you trifled with. She was the kind of woman who deserved to be treasured, cherished. And committing himself to Lazy L was about as dedicated as he was prepared to get these days.

She was still hurt by what had happened in the first place, he could tell. No matter what she *thought* had happened, she'd be wrong. And he had no energy to explain it to her, to see the look of disappointment and dismay on her pretty, generous face. It had been difficult enough, saying as much as he had about his mother. Seeing the look of pity pass across her face. Oh, she'd tried to hide it, but it had been there. She'd felt sorry for him. And pity wasn't what he wanted from her.

He'd spent a long day leveling the drive with a rented grader and fixing fences out in the quarter section, while the crew of students he'd hired had finished painting the barn. The progress over the last week was mind-boggling, but the dance was tomorrow and the electrician had just finished wiring up the clinical area at the front of the building. There was still equipment to install, supplies to unpack. The rented sound equipment to set up for the dance. Tonight he was bone-weary. And wondering if he was turning into some crackpot idealist trying to do this thing.

He went to the bathroom to wash his hands. A jar of cinnamon-smelling potpourri sat on the tiny vanity, and a cheerful cherry-red handtowel hung from the round towel hook. Such small touches and even the tiny half-bath looked welcoming.

Hell, even the loft was transformed. He'd heard the syncopated sound of a staple gun and had returned to the barn tonight to see ropes of white mini-lights strung along the rafters and down the stair railing. Along one long wall she'd already set up the church banquet tables and laid them with white and red plaid cloths. He had no idea where they'd come from. The straw bales that had been downstairs were now upstairs, at right angles to the stage, artistically placed with a pitchfork next to one and an old saddle over the other. She'd lugged the heavy bales up there herself, he'd realized with wonder.

Long benches, something he thought would be more likely in an old schoolroom than his barn, lined the other wall as seating. She'd even thought to put a bucket of sand near the stage for the dance floor.

She was a miracle worker, and he tried very hard to resent her for it. But he couldn't. Because she was Jen, his Jen, who had always had a way of making people feel good simply by being around them. She was the kind of woman people relied upon, no matter what. A constant. It was no wonder the people of the town rallied around her.

Right now his stomach was speaking louder than his conscience. He put a dish of the lasagna she'd left behind in the oven to heat. Tomorrow her official job would be done and the dance would be over. The work on Lazy L Rescue Ranch would begin. He'd settle up with her—adding in extra for her efforts in the house and barn—and they could go back to being contemporaries. No, friends. That was all.

That was all he had to offer. It was all he could expect. He certainly wouldn't become her lover. Even if he couldn't get her smoky eyes or her wistful smile out of his mind.

CHAPTER SIX

THE Christensen Brothers were warming up in the barn and the twinkle lights were glowing faintly as the sun started its descent in the cool spring sky. Andrew greeted guests in the yard, directing the parking. He hadn't expected this good a turnout. Neighbors, old friends, townspeople were all arriving; ranchers and business owners shook his hand and asked questions about his venture. The smile he'd forced onto his face now stayed there all on its own. Normally he kept to himself, only socializing within the industry when called upon to do so and never hosting. But this didn't have the affectation he had become used to. It was friends and neighbors and a level of comfort he was surprised to encounter.

This was going to work. And his hope was that in it he'd find the satisfaction that had somehow been missing all these years. Tonight he felt as if he was *where he belonged*.

Jen passed him, going from kitchen to barn, throwing a smile in his direction. The warmth in her eyes made his heart thump and he tried to push it aside. She only wanted to be neighborly. It was who she was, he realized. He knew without a doubt that she'd be doing the same thing for anyone who'd asked for help—she was that kind of warm, giving person. It was one of the things he liked most about her.

And yet as he watched her walk away, in a pair of faded jeans, he couldn't forget the way she'd felt pressed against him when they'd kissed at Snickerdoodles. She'd gone above and beyond getting ready for tonight. He wished there was a way he could return the favor. He knew she had to be struggling with the bakery. It wasn't easy, running a small business. Once things got settled he'd think of something as a thank-you.

"Andrew!"

A familiar voice calling his name drew his attention back from its meanderings. It was Lucy, followed by Brody and Betty Polcyk. Lucy's red hair rioted around her glowing face, and as she came forward to give him a hug her firm belly made a round barrier between their bodies. He laughed, kissed her cheek and stood back. "You look wonderful."

She looked down at herself and shrugged. "I look like an apple," she replied, but grabbed his hand and pressed it against the warm mound. "Look at this. Junior's ready to dance."

He had no time to react. His hand was placed on the crest of her belly and he felt several strong kicks against his palm. His eyes stared at the spot…dear Lord, he could actually see her stomach change shape. He was used to this in mares, but not in women. It had a way of humbling a man, even one who was just an old friend.

He tried a laugh. "He's already doing a two-step in there!"

Brody came up behind Lucy and put his hands on her shoulders. "I told her she had to take it easy. But she's determined to dance."

"And you never argue with a pregnant woman."

Jen's teasing voice came from behind Andrew and everyone chuckled. He slid his hand away, a bit reluctantly. He'd never felt an actual baby move beneath his hand before, and the miracle wasn't lost on him.

He tried to imagine Gerald touching his mother like this,

but the picture wouldn't gel. The old man had held so much resentment for so long that he couldn't conjure up fantasies of marital bliss. Gerald had never been one to show affection, not to his wife and not to Andrew. But Brody and Lucy—Andrew smiled. This was how it should be.

He watched helplessly as Jen came forward and gave Lucy a quick hug. He swallowed hard. As teenagers they'd whispered in the dark about the kids they'd have someday, never imagining how far apart life would take them. Hell, he remembered one time when Brody's dad had thrown his annual dance and Brody had found him and Jen in a dark corner of the barn. Brody had teased him, saying Andrew and Jen would have a houseful of kids before he even got started. The memory of sneaking moments with her sent a rush of desire through him. Now they were all grown up, and it was Brody preparing for fatherhood. Andrew and Jen struggled to have an uncomplicated conversation at the best of times. Memories kept getting in the way.

Andrew stepped back, lifting a hand. "I'll see you all later. Have fun." He had other people to greet. And he had to stop letting the past take over. Look at Jen. She'd dusted herself off and carried on splendidly without him.

When the yard was full, and the cars had started lining up along the road, Andrew made his way to the loft to join the festivities. The floor was already vibrating with the stomping of feet and the pulse of the bass guitar and drums as the Christensens whooped it up.

The noise was raucous, and people he knew—and many he didn't—shouted to be heard over the band and others talking. A young girl bustled around the banquet tables, cleaning up empty plates and napkins, replenishing the paper goods, and organizing the platters as guests nibbled at the food Jen had prepared. Agnes Dodds waltzed past with Tom Walker, who'd owned the feed store before passing the reins to his son, Tom Junior. She threw an outrageous wink in his direction and he laughed, winking back. Some things in Larch Valley never changed at all. Sometimes he found it aggravating, like being under the microscope at the pizza parlor, but on a night like tonight he could see how that was just as it should be.

Jen returned, carrying a platter of what he recognized as Southwest Spirals and chicken and cheese taquitos. As much as he didn't want to admit it, she'd changed. She had grown into an independent, confident woman. Successful, beautiful, beloved by the town. She was happy. Once she'd told him her fears and wishes. But they'd made their lives without each other. He watched her work, smiling and chatting to neighbors as her hands flew over the trays. It wasn't just memories pushing him now. He was starting to care for the strong, independent woman she'd become.

She was talking to the girl behind the table when he approached. "This looks great, Jen. You've outdone yourself."

She smiled her brilliant smile and it caught him square in the gut. Lord, when she smiled like that it lit up a whole room. "Have you met Suzanne? She's a local girl, graduating this year."

He held out his hand and Suzanne looked up at him, wide-eyed. She took his hand and shook it, then smiled with a mouth full of braces. He couldn't help it. His own grin widened. "Thanks for helping out tonight, Suzanne."

Jen saved the poor girl from gawking. "Suzanne is going to wait tables this summer at the café, and help with the catering."

The band broke into a rowdy two-step, and Andrew's toe started tapping. "You're doing a great job," he called to the teen. "Could you spare your boss for a dance?"

He turned his gaze to Jen, who had just finished pulling the plastic wrap off a platter. "Me?"

"Care to take those boots for a spin, Miss O'Keefe?" He raised an eyebrow, challenging. Daring.

For a moment he thought she was going to refuse. But Suzanne nudged her arm and took the plastic from her fingers. "Go on, I'll be fine."

"O…Okay."

He held out his hand and she took it, coming around the corner of the table.

Her palm was warm and soft in his, and his chest constricted at the sight of her, slightly in front of him, in a pair of well-worn jeans that looked as if they'd been made for her figure. She wore a black form-fitting T-shirt that said "Snickerdoodles" on the left chest, in printing that matched the sign above her store. When she turned to him and placed her hand inside his, he placed his right hand on her waist. It felt warm and lean beneath his palm.

Maybe this was a mistake. A really big one. Because touching was touching, and it had the same affect on him no matter if it was in a room full of neighbors stomping to music or in a quiet, empty bakery late at night.

Jen fought to keep her smile in place and her hand in his as his grin faded and he stared into her eyes. What had she done now? Unless his touching her was causing the same internal reaction to him as it did to her. The moment she'd turned and assumed the dance position there'd been a change. Facing him was too much like when she'd fallen off the ladder straight into his arms. It made her chest hurt from breathing fast and shallow, made her body tingle from remembering being flush against his. And now it felt as if half the town was watching them.

For the first time in forever Jen wished she wasn't in a place where everyone knew her secrets. Everyone remembered that Jen and Andrew had been high school sweethearts. Everyone remembered how she'd mourned the loss of him. She knew that they couldn't even have a simple dance without there being speculation.

"Stop looking at me like that," she said, as low as she possibly could.

"What?"

And still their feet refused to move. She saw two more pairs of eyes dance past them, curiously peering over shoulders to see what was going on. She couldn't possibly repeat herself any louder. She put back her shoulders and lifted her chin. "Just dance with me, will you?"

He heard the command and picked up the beat, leading her backward at last. The motion of the dance at least kept their bodies from brushing too much, and after going around the floor once Jen started to relax. She had been staring at a point past his shoulder, feeling awkward. But the rousing music did its job, and before long she found herself enjoying it. He was a good dancer, smooth and confident. It seemed the simplest thing in the world when he looped her under his arm and back again.

She stopped staring beyond him and shifted her eyes to his face.

It was as if no time had elapsed at all. His gaze was warm beneath his favorite well-worn Stetson, his eyes laughing at her as their feet glided smoothly over the boards. A tan-colored shirt flowed over his broad shoulders, the color picking up the gold flecks in his hazel eyes. He was filled out, a more mature version of the boy she'd known, but he moved the same. Smelled the same. Heavens, he even felt the same, she realized as his hand tightened on hers like it had the dozens of times they'd danced before.

This bigger, broader, older Drew was far more dangerous than the boy she remembered.

The two-step ended, but Andrew didn't release her hand. "One more." He leaned forward and said it in her ear.

"I should get back…"

"Your helper can manage for five more minutes," he insisted.

She wanted to. She was beginning to realize that the attraction buzzing through her veins was based very little on the past and had much more to do with the man before her now. It made him seem like a familiar stranger, one who knew her better than most and yet someone so completely brand new that she was drawn to him. At first she'd only wanted to know why he'd gone, and had put up walls, trying to protect herself from the pain. When had that changed? When had she stopped being so angry? Now she craved to know about all the years in between. About the man before her now, who had made such a right-angle turn in the path of his life.

It was complicated. Despite the kiss, he hadn't said a single word about wanting to pick up where they'd left off. Not that they could. But she could have one more dance, here in front of lots of people, where nothing would happen. *Five minutes*. A safe five minutes, where she could be held in his arms and pretend. She would allow herself that.

A fiddle began to scrape and Jen heard the beginnings of a waltz. Deep inside, energy raced through her as they altered their hold and their bodies brushed. After tonight she wouldn't have the excuse of the job to see him anymore. They would only run into each other occasionally in town. As she held her breath and felt his chest touch hers, she knew she would miss him.

Their feet made shuffling sounds in the thin layer of sand that skimmed the floor. The fiddle sang out a lonesome tune to the one-two-three rhythm, creating an ache in her heart. As she let out a sigh, Drew's arm tightened around her, drawing her even closer. The backs of her eyelids stung. It was almost as if he were saying *I'm sorry* with his body. But that was silly, wasn't it? She was sure he wasn't sorry at all. She was just being fanciful.

Their feet took smaller and smaller steps, and her head rested against his strong shoulder. In a few minutes the music would stop and he'd walk away. She wouldn't be able to feel the muscle beneath her cheek, or smell his scent that was an individual cocktail of man and hay and soap, or hear the way his voice said her name softly, with the slightest bit of hoarseness in it, like sandpaper.

Like he did now.

"Jen."

She turned her head to look up at him and he looked down, his lips a firm line but his eyes a tangle of emotion. Her left foot stumbled and he righted her with one strong arm. For a bar of music everything seemed to hold, suspended. Then he lifted their joined hands so they were clasped between them and dipped his head to kiss her.

The song, the voices, the sound of boots on the wood floor all dissolved into a pleasant hum as Jen focused on the feel and taste of his mouth on hers. His fingers gripped almost painfully around hers, and she moved her opposite hand from his shoulder to curl it around his back, her fingertips grazing the short strands of his hairline beneath the hat.

This kiss was different than the last. This was a hello— light, soft, firm, and warm all at once. She didn't have to know the reasons to know that somehow she'd forgiven him. It didn't matter. What mattered was the man before her now. A man who had returned to face his demons, who wanted to resurrect Lazy L into something good. Who kissed like an angel.

Her heart tripped as he sighed into her mouth. She wanted to melt against him. To…

And then, like a thunder crash, she remembered where

they were. In the space of a second she realized the music had stopped and that the barn was utterly silent. She stepped back, breaking off the kiss but unable to tear her gaze from his. His hands lowered and hung loosely by his sides, and a small, teasing smile flirted with the corner of his mouth, as if to say *our secret's out now*.

But she didn't feel like teasing. A hurried glance around her told her that every single person there was watching with morbid fascination. The blush started at her chest and worked its way north to her face in an instant, and she pressed her hands to her cheeks. Oh, Lord, what had they done?

As Andrew started to chuckle, so did the closest dancers to them, and before long most everyone was laughing and clapping.

Jen's heart tumbled. She felt utterly exposed, but she knew she had two options. Cut him and run, or pretend to join in the good-natured feeling and pretend it was no big deal. The last thing she wanted was to make a scene. She forced her lips to curve and delivered a mock curtsey to Andrew, who laughed and reached out for her hand. She let him tuck her under his arm for a few moments as they provided a unified front. But the smile felt brittle, and inside she was trembling. How could he have done that, in front of everyone? And why? She'd done a lot of recovering under the watchful eyes of the town. It felt wrong, working through those feelings in such a public way.

"I need to get back to work." She stood on tiptoe and said it in Andrew's ear as the music started up again.

He nodded and smiled, his hand resting along the small of her back just a little bit longer than she was comfortable with. "We'll talk later."

Their heads were close enough that his hat hid Jen's next expression. "Count on it," she replied quietly, then spun back to the buffet table to hide her flushed cheeks.

* * *

He had to be seven kinds of fool, kissing her like that.

Andrew avoided her for the rest of the night, instead talking to ranchers and business owners about the rescue ranch project and disappearing now and then to do an impromptu tour. Still, every time he turned a corner or returned to the loft and the dance, he looked for her. She'd felt so right in his arms. And the way she'd looked up at him... He'd just done it on impulse. Kissed her. Like a teenager at a school dance.

What had happened to the whole "pay her and go their separate ways" idea he'd promised himself just yesterday? She might fit in his arms like a puzzle piece, and kiss like an angel, but he couldn't let things go too far. She'd ask questions he didn't ever want to answer. He'd come home for a clean slate. He would have to apologize. Take a step back.

He danced with Lucy twice, and even with Agnes Dodds. She watched him with a sharp eye. "Young man," she stated clearly as he took small steps in deference to her stature, "you better not be toying with that girl."

Clearly he hadn't been thinking at all. Because every single person in this room knew he and Jen had history. And if they hadn't known it before they sure knew it now. The tongues were wagging. He had forgotten what it was like here. For Pete's sake, the town would have them walking down the aisle before the night was over. A simple mistaken kiss would create all sorts of mischief.

And yet there wasn't much simple about it. His eyes kept seeking her out, no matter where she was. Presently, as he danced with the wife of a neighboring rancher, he found Jen across the room, replenishing a platter. He felt his heart twist as she smiled at a guest. Why was it that, as much as he told himself he shouldn't, he found himself going back to her time and again? Wanting to tell her secrets?

He hovered by the barn door in the cool air as the dancing

reached a fever pitch. The evening, as far as the Lazy L went, had been a resounding success.

He shook hands and thanked people for coming, but a big surprise came when Clay Gregory, a nearby neighbor, made to leave.

"Thanks for coming, Clay."

"You got it. You know you can count on me for a spare set of hands, Andrew."

"Appreciate it." Andrew shifted his eyes, but Clay, who was more than a match for Andrew's own size and strength, didn't move on.

"Don't mess with Jen," Clay warned.

Andrew looked back. Clay's expression was as mild and relaxed as before, but the steel in his dark eyes told Drew he was serious. "I wouldn't."

Clay took a step back. "That's good. I'm not sure she could take it again."

Clay left, but Andrew's mind was working double-time. What on earth…? First Agnes, who he could see meddling because everyone knew she was a bit of a busybody. But Clay? He hadn't acted like he was jealous, either. More like…more like a big brother.

Kissing Jen had been a bigger mistake than he'd realized. He had been gone too long. And he knew if there were sides to be taken the whole of Larch Valley would line up behind her.

As a line of guilt snuck through him, he suddenly realized Jen wasn't the only one who had a right to a grudge. And, more than ever, he felt the walls of the town close around him—much as they had several springs ago.

Jen hadn't danced after the kiss—not even with Brody when he'd asked. She was there to do a job and that was exactly what she was going to do. To the mothers, grandmothers and starry-eyed lovers she mentioned weddings and babies and showers. To the local business owners she promoted the catering side of Snickerdoodles for functions and parties. That was the real reason she'd agreed to take the job tonight. She had to remember that.

Andrew spun by with a woman hanging on his every word, and Jen snapped the lid on a container firmly. She had a bank loan stating she had to make a go of this expansion. She had to keep her eye on the prize. None of this dreaming and romanticizing. This time she didn't have Gerald to co-sign the loan. Instead she'd had to put her house up as collateral.

Shortly after eleven, Andrew made a speech. Jen took the precious minutes to give herself a break, and she opened a bottle of water and perched on a bale of straw. He welcomed everyone, and then outlined his reasons for converting Lazy L into a rescue ranch. He was passionate, but not overly so, convincing without being preachy. Asking for help without begging. And her respect for him—as a rancher and as a man—went up a few notches.

But when he ended by thanking those who had already committed to helping, and then moved on to thank the Christensen Brothers for providing the music, her heart froze. *Don't thank me*, she thought. It would be the beginning of what that kiss had meant, and she despised it.

His gaze turned her way. *Please don't thank me*, she pleaded silently.

"And another big thank-you to Jen O'Keefe, for helping with the decorations and providing the food tonight." Appraising looks focused her way, and she gritted her teeth beneath the professional smile she had to produce. "Jen's expanding Snickerdoodles, so I know you'll all want to grab a flyer and see what's happening with her Main Avenue location."

She wanted to sink through the floor. This was worse than

she'd imagined. She'd wanted to cater tonight to get a jump in advertising, to get the word out. But not this way. Because everyone looking at her now didn't see Jen O'Keefe, business owner, standing on her own two feet. They saw that kiss.

She knew enough about Larch Valley to know that once a collective opinion had been formed it would take an earthquake to move it again. Everyone would be convinced that Andrew had hired her for personal reasons, not professional. She closed her eyes briefly, trying to think of the best way to handle things.

As Andrew encouraged everyone to have a good time through the final set, she steeled her spine. What was done was done, and she couldn't change it even if she did desperately want to take it back. What hadn't changed was her objective. She was Jen O'Keefe, doing a job, and that was what she would do. Anything else she was—real or imagined— would have to wait.

And once the last car was gone she'd clear the air with Andrew once and for all.

CHAPTER SEVEN

JEN carefully avoided Andrew until the last stragglers were packing it in. She sent Suzanne home and started tidying the mess herself. The table and counters were a mass of dirty dishes, empty containers and scattered lids. The pristine order and organization before the event had disintegrated into empty chaos, right along with her good intentions. But, like the dance, the adrenaline rush of earlier had worn off, the end was a let-down, and she wished she didn't have to take the energy to clean it up. At least the food had been a hit. Most of what she was packing in her car now was empty platters and containers, not leftovers.

She was washing out an empty chafing dish when Andrew opened the screen door and the last truck departed with a honk of the horn.

Her feet ached, there was a definite pounding beginning behind her temples, and right now nothing sounded better than a hot bath and a soft bed.

But they had things to talk about first, and if they didn't do it now she'd lie awake fretting over it all night. Sleep was too precious a commodity to waste.

"You're angry." His deep voice echoed through the kitchen, but he came no further than his spot just inside the door. How many times had she stood in this kitchen since he'd gone away, hoping he'd walk back through it? Now he had—but not for the reason she'd once wished for.

She took a deep breath and let it out, because she badly felt like snapping at him, or being sarcastic, and neither would be beneficial.

"I am, yes. And confused."

"Which one most?"

He stayed where he was, as if waiting for her answer would make up his mind if he should come in or not, despite it being his house. She rubbed the scoring pad over the steel with renewed vigor. Angry, yes, but perhaps not for the reason he thought.

Her hand paused in the dishwater. She half turned, faced him to answer his question. He still stood by the door, one hand resting on a dining chair. He had taken his hat off and the top spiky part of his hair was slightly flattened where it had rested.

"Why did you do it, Drew? In front of everyone?"

"I don't know." He shrugged, dismissing the question.

"Sure you do," she persisted, noting that he'd shoved his hands into his pockets the way a small boy would when he got caught out.

"Maybe I got swept up in the moment."

She snorted softly and turned her attention back to the dish, scrubbing out dried-on bits of food.

"You don't believe me?"

"Believe that your brain suddenly left your body? No, I don't. Don't you know how it looked when you thanked me like that?"

"This is about my *speech*?"

There was no way he could fake the tone of surprise, and she abandoned the dishes, turning to face him. "What did you think I was angry about?"

The air hummed.

The answer floated through the kitchen even without words. Finally Jen said it, so softly it was barely louder than the hum from the lightbulb above their heads.

"You thought I was angry about the kiss." Even as she said it her insides curled with remembrance of how his lips felt on hers, the vibration of his body against her as he held her close.

"Aren't you?" He started to step forward, but then seemed to think better of it.

Was she? Yes and no. How could she be angry when she'd wanted to kiss him in the first place? And yet…

"I wish you hadn't done it in front of everyone, that's all. It created a scene."

Finally he stepped further into the room, his lazy stride easily eating up the feet between them. "It was just a kiss."

Jen lifted her face up to his. "It might have been to you."

"Are you saying it meant something?"

His eyebrows lifted. His face was a blank of innocence. Was he really so oblivious to her growing feelings for him? Her heart sank, heavy with disappointment. Clearly, while her feelings had grown his had not, or he wouldn't dismiss it in such a way or be so surprised.

He was too close; she backed away and put up her hands. "That is not what I meant. This isn't even about you and me now. It's about…about…" Her arm swept wide, as if encompassing the whole valley.

"You're worried what people will think? After one little kiss?"

The dimple in his cheek popped ever so slightly and his shoulders relaxed. He reached out and touched her cheek with one finger. "Don't worry, Jen, it'll be forgotten tomorrow."

"No, it won't. Don't you see?" She jerked her head away from his touch and grabbed a dishtowel, wiping the remaining moisture from her hands. "This isn't some big city party where people hook up one night and go their separate ways the next. You should know. The valley doesn't have that—well, what you would call level of sophistication. They didn't see a kiss at a dance. They saw two of its own with a history, smooching on the dance floor. They saw you putting your mark on me in front of everyone. And then when you thanked me…don't you see how it looked? I didn't want *us* in the spotlight."

"So which is bothering you? The fact that it was in public, or the fact that I kissed you at all? Believe me, I've already been warned against hurting you again."

Heat blossomed in her cheeks and she avoided his steady gaze. The truth was she *had* wanted him to kiss her. She hadn't been able to stop thinking about it, even when she was painting or filling out purchase orders or lining up catering jobs.

She skirted around him and started matching plastic containers with lids. "So why did you? Really?"

This time he looked away. He didn't answer for several seconds.

"I did get swept away. With you in my arms, and the way your hand felt in mine, and your cheek resting on my shoulder… Dammit, woman, I'm not made of stone. I wanted to kiss you and I did."

She swallowed against the lump in her throat as her hands stilled. He was right in that the dance had spawned something between them that was irrefutable. Why had she let him hold her so close? Or put her cheek against him, closing her eyes? She was as much to blame. And now she didn't know what was real and what was fantasy.

"I can't do this, Drew." She knew she'd forgiven him for leaving all those years ago, but that didn't mean she'd forgotten how it had hurt, or that she was willing to set herself up again. And Andrew had *complication* written all over him. She couldn't afford to lose focus on the big picture. This time she had to use her head.

He came forward and put his hands on her upper arms, his fingers warm and sure. "Think about it, Jen. I've been back a few weeks and we keep having these conversations. I keep kissing you. You keep kissing me back. What does that tell you?"

"It tells me I need to stop being in the same room with you, that's what." She shrugged off his hands and gathered up the empty pans to take back to her house.

"It tells me we're not over," he replied, putting a large hand over her wrist, stopping her movements.

But it was exactly what Jen needed to hear. All the resentment she'd been carrying for over a decade was suddenly diffused, floating away on the night air, leaving her feeling strangely empty. Maybe Drew really needed to understand how he'd hurt her. Maybe then he'd realize why forgiving wasn't the same as forgetting.

"Oh, but we *are* over," she said sadly, twisting her wrist free and putting the pans together in a precise stack. "And you made sure of that. You sealed that deal when you made the choice not to come back."

"I am back."

"Twelve years is a tad bit late, in my opinion."

He ran a hand over his hair. "I had my reasons."

"Oh, I'm sure you did." She picked up the pans and headed for the door, balancing them and pulling the screen door open with one hand. She carefully descended the verandah steps and walked to her car. She heard his boots following her and sighed. "I'm not interested in your reasons. You promised me. You promised you'd…"

But words failed her as the lump returned in her throat, rendering her speechless. He'd promised her she'd never be alone, but he'd left her alone. That was exactly what he'd done. And then he'd turned his back on the one person who'd actually shown any faith in her. Gerald. He'd hurt both of them so badly.

"I promised to come back." His voice was low and filled with regret. She opened the back door to her car and put the pans inside, closing her eyes for a moment to gather strength. She shut it again, and forced herself to look at him as the wall of anger she'd erected long ago crumbled into dust.

"No, Drew. You promised you wouldn't leave me alone. But that's what you did. Less than a year after we graduated Mum and Dad moved to Lethbridge, so Dad could be closer to the hospital. They signed over the deed to the house to me, but I was on my own."

"Why didn't you just go with them?"

He really didn't get it. The words hovered on her tongue but she couldn't say them. And then he spoke again, this time his words harsh and sharp as knives.

"You could have come with me. I asked you to."

"My life was here." She folded her arms across her middle, trying to keep warm in the chilly air, trying to protect herself and her core of hurt. Anything to keep him at a distance.

"And mine wasn't. You made your choice. Why is yours okay and mine wrong?"

"Because here was *home*! Why didn't you come back? You had Lazy L. Noah and Gerald. And me!" She lifted her chin as she felt tears spurt into her eyes, saying all the things she'd wanted to say for so long.

His lips twisted, as if he was in pain. "I couldn't. I just couldn't."

"Why? Don't I deserve to know why, after all this time? After what happened tonight? Do you want to know why tonight was different? Because those people were there for me when you left the first time. They remember." She shivered, suddenly feeling the evening chill. "I mourned you, Drew." Two tears gathered in the corners of her eyes slid down her cheeks. "The people of Larch Valley saw me with a broken heart. And they were there for me when I put it back together. If we're going to resolve what's between us, can't you understand that I'd rather not do it with the whole of Larch Valley looking on?"

"If you want me to apologize, I will. For the timing. I realized it right away. I'd forgotten what Larch Valley was like."

He wasn't apologizing for the actual kiss, and knowing it sent her pulse racing. She was so afraid to repeat past mistakes, and yet so attracted to the man before her now. "Who was it that warned you off? I think I'd like to know."

"Agnes and Clay."

Jen indulged in a small affectionate smile. Agnes was a gem and Clay was a good man. "So you know what I mean. For you to kiss me like that, after how hard I've worked to stand on my own—" She broke off, choking on the words. Her feelings for him were new and yet old, bound up in a history she couldn't erase. "You thanked me for catering, but you made it seem personal and not professional."

"I was only trying to make it up to you."

"Then help me put this behind us. I don't want to live with the past hanging over me any longer. With unanswered questions plaguing my mind. I want to move on. I've worked so hard to move on. So please, Drew. Put me out of my misery and just tell me *why* you left and never came back until your father's funeral."

The moon was behind him, casting a pale glow against his form. The night was cool enough that their breath made tiny puffs of cloud in front of their faces. And Drew looked like a haunted man, the hollows of his cheeks in sharp relief in the shadows, his eyes dark with pain.

"He wasn't my father."

Jen's heart dropped clear to her toes. She must have heard wrong. "What do you mean?" she whispered. Drew's face was in utter earnest. "What do you mean, he wasn't your father?"

"Gerald Laramie wasn't my father. I'm not a Laramie at all."

He spun on his heel and went back to the house. Jen stood for a moment beside her car, her mouth hanging open. For a fleeting second she considered getting behind the wheel and driving away.

But she couldn't. She couldn't drive away from the look of anguish on his face, from the man who had made her laugh, the one who had sent her heart soaring with a kiss. So she made the long walk back to the house and the man she was trying very hard not to fall in love with all over again.

Andrew's heart clubbed against his ribs as he walked away from her and back to the house. He couldn't believe he'd actually said it. Out loud. To *her*. Maybe it was for the best. There wouldn't be any more pretending. And she'd understand why he had felt he couldn't come home.

He never should have kissed her. He never should have come back here, he realized. It was too painful. He should have sold Lazy L, taken his half of the profits and set up shop somewhere else. Whoever the hell had said you could always come back home again needed a smack upside the head. It didn't solve anything. It just made life that much more mixed up.

He paced in the dark living room for a while. A broken heart? Had she really said that? It seemed impossible. He'd known she'd be hurt, but he hadn't realized the full extent. Now he could add that particular regret to his list of unresolved feelings.

He listened for the sound of Jen's engine and her car peeling out the driveway. It never came. Instead, he heard her footsteps on the verandah.

She came to stand in the doorway, leaning one shoulder against the frame, her eyes soft with understanding. How could that be, when she'd just told him how much he'd hurt her? Her ponytail had little bits coming out and they framed her face, adding a delicious softness. When they'd been dating he'd teased her by pulling out her elastic and running his fingers through her hair. He wished life were that simple again. But it wasn't. Never would be again.

"You should have told me," she whispered.

"I never told anyone."

"And neither did Gerald. I'm sure of it." She stayed where she was, but he detected a shimmer of tension in her posture. She had a soft spot where his father—where *Gerald*—was concerned. She hadn't seen him the way Andrew had.

"He sure made a point of telling *me*."

He heard the pain in his voice and hated it. It made him feel weak. Nothing was easy these days. Not even the anger he'd been carrying around since he was a teen.

"Are you going to tell me what happened, or am I going to have to pry it out of you?"

"Does it matter? I'm not Gerald's son."

"Gerald was good to me, especially when everyone else seemed to have disappeared." She boosted herself away from the doorframe. "So, yes, it matters."

She was right. They kept saying one thing and doing another. Keeping it professional but letting personal stuff creep in. What was the alternative? Love? Commitment? With Jen there would be nothing less.

And he couldn't give it to her. What they needed to do was talk it out so she could finally be free. Perhaps if she knew the truth it would make sense.

"You were the best thing about high school, you know that?" He took a step toward her but stopped, unsure of whether or not he should touch her again. How could he possibly make her understand when he didn't even quite get it? "And the one good thing about coming home. Maybe that's why I keep hanging around. Because you're the one person who doesn't make me feel like a stranger in my own hometown."

"Then why did you come back? Why here?"

He wanted to touch her but was afraid. And if he held her now that wouldn't really help with the "set her free" part. He sighed. It was a damnable thing, wanting to hold a woman and yet knowing you were both better off if you didn't.

"Let's sit down."

He went to the sofa and sat, resting his elbows on his knees and rubbing his hands through his hair a few times. He felt rather than saw her sit on the couch beside him, saw her smaller boots next to his bigger ones, and smiled a sad smile.

"The truth, then," he conceded. "I had to come here," he admitted. "I felt I had something to prove, and I knew that here was where I had to prove it. At Lazy L."

"A connection?"

"Maybe."

"It was here for you all along."

"No, I'm not sure it was." He leaned back against the cushions and closed his eyes. He couldn't stand to see the sympathy on her face. "When I told Gerald I wanted to go away to school, to study and be a vet, he was so angry. Noah had already gone to boot camp, remember? And I didn't say anything until after I'd applied for pre-vet. He was furious. He wanted me to take over the ranch, you see. And I didn't want it. I was seventeen and I wanted to make my own way, not be stuck on the family farm for the rest of my life." He sighed, remembering the arguments. "I was cruel, and I said things. Oh, it wasn't so much that I said them, but how I did. One night the arguing got really heated, and I said I wished I wasn't his son. And he told me I wasn't."

"Oh, Drew."

The world had a hard brittle edge just now, and Andrew clenched his teeth against it. "I goaded him into it. But that wasn't the worst of it, Jen."

She reached over and took his hand in hers. He squeezed it, knowing that once she heard the rest her simple comfort would be taken away.

"He was the one that sent my mother away. He forced her to leave by saying he'd take her to court with a drawn-out custody battle. That by the end everyone would know what kind of a woman she was."

Jen gave a little gasp. Gerald would never have done such a thing! It certainly didn't gel with her memories of a man who'd been kind and supportive, who'd even co-signed her first business loan. Or the man who had missed his son and followed his career with pride. "Why would he do that? I can't believe it, Andrew."

Andrew's hand was still in hers, and she kept the connection. She knew he believed what he was saying, but he had to be mistaken. She couldn't believe Gerald would be so cruel as to take a mother away from her children.

"He did it because she was having another affair. I'd been the product of the previous one."

It seemed incredible. Things like this—sordid affairs and tawdry goings-on—just didn't happen in Larch Valley. Her heart seemed to pause for a minute as she asked, "Do you know who your real father is?"

He shook his head. "No, only that he was already married. And that he wasn't from the valley."

It almost seemed as if the world she knew was falling down, like a tower of blocks tumbling to the ground. "I don't know what to say."

"I didn't either. I was barely five when she left us, but I had memories of her. Good ones. He never let us talk about her, but Noah had heard arguments. He'd told me things that didn't make sense then but did as I got older. When I asked Gerald why she didn't take us with her he said she didn't want to split us up, and that Noah was his."

Her fingers trembled inside his cold grip at what the words implied—how he must have interpreted them. How destroying for a boy to hear that. Both about his mother's infidelity and then affirming that he didn't belong. She forgot about Gerald for the moment, and focused only on Drew's pain. "You must have felt awful. Unwanted."

"I felt like a consequence."

His voice broke on the last word and Jen scooted over, tucking her legs up on the sofa and curling against his side. "Oh, Drew," she said again, profoundly sad for the boy who'd lost his innocence. It didn't have to make sense for her to understand how deeply he'd been hurt.

"I tried for years to prove to him that I'd made the right decision. I studied hard so I'd be top of my class. I invited him to my graduation but he didn't come. I sent clippings of places I'd been, things I'd done. But nothing seemed to move him. I looked back and remembered how he'd never told me he loved me, not even as a boy. I wasn't his, Jen. I couldn't face coming home. I hated home. And I couldn't tell you."

"Why ever not? I loved you." She whispered it in the dark. A part of her mourned for what he'd lost; another part felt betrayed that he hadn't shared it with her. Had he felt ashamed? Angry? She wouldn't have cared a bit about it. She would have held him, and kissed him, consoled him as best she could. They might have been young, but for her those feelings had been real. It hurt to know perhaps his hadn't been as sincere as she'd thought.

"I thought you left because of me."

"No—never!" He turned a bit and she felt his hard gaze on her face. "But I was too ashamed to tell you. I was nothing. I was some bastard boy who'd turned out to be a disappointment. That was what he said. The valley became a place with walls that seemed to close in more every day. I couldn't stay."

"If you'd told me…"

"What? You would have gone with me?"

The question stabbed into her conscience. She would have understood, commiserated, petted. But would she have packed up and gone with him? "I don't know. Maybe if I'd understood…"

"I asked you to come. You kept saying you couldn't leave your father. You said your place was with your family."

His words opened a hollow space inside her. "Dad was sick. I couldn't just up and leave. I was so afraid if I did something would happen…"

"Can't you see how different or situations were? You were dedicated to your father and I suddenly didn't have one. When you refused me, that was it. I had to cut ties." Andrew pushed his way off the couch, leaving her sitting there alone.

Jen stared at his back. He'd understood how she loved her father but had felt eclipsed by his illness, felt like he was always in the background. For two years Drew had put her first. Listened to her, had fun with her when laughter was scarce. Had loved her.

Now that a piece of the puzzle was in place, she was starting to understand. Suddenly forgiving him seemed easier. How could she condemn a boy who'd had to face such a devastating truth?

"Did you ever try talking to him again? If you'd talked to him you would have realized how much he loved you. His talk of regrets makes sense now. He was so proud of you! He told me all the time about things you'd done in your career."

Andrew looked as if someone had ripped the earth from beneath his feet. "What are you talking about? I lived with Gerald my whole life. Words of love…of pride…that's not the man I knew. Lord knows I tried!"

"Tried how?"

Drew rubbed a hand over his mouth. "Letters. Articles, pictures. Even my university transcripts."

Jen wrinkled her brow. So much of it didn't make sense, and now Gerald was gone perhaps they would never have the answers. Maybe all she could do was try to make it easier for him. "All I know is that the man I knew was gutted that you never came home. He could have sold this place a million times but he didn't. He left it to his *sons*. Plural, Drew. Hang on to that. He did love you. I'm sure of it."

"And yet here I am, still trying to prove something. To a ghost."

The fact that he was still trying, the fact that he was hurting so deeply touched her, but she hadn't gone through heartbreak without it opening her eyes a whole lot wider. Drew had so much to work through on his own, things that had nothing to do with her. She could see that now. What would happen when he figured it out? Would he leave again? She just wasn't up to being collateral damage once more. She couldn't willingly set herself up to be hurt twice.

What Drew was dealing with now was bigger than her feelings for him. Feelings she hadn't necessarily wanted but that seemed to be growing all the time. And she couldn't trust his perspective either. He was going through so much. She was here and she was familiar, something for him to hold on to. Once he'd worked through the rest of his problems he might discover she wasn't what he wanted anyway. He would put her in the past, just like he would his father.

He could never know how much she was starting to care

again. Her heart ached for the whole convoluted situation as tears slipped down her cheeks.

"I only know that from my perspective Gerald loved you. Was proud of you."

Drew's tortured expression was more than she could bear.

"And so am I," she whispered brokenly, and before he could say more, she ran from the room, out the door and to her car.

She wiped her hand across her face, clearing the tears as she drove away. Maybe it was good that they'd finally cleared the air about the past. Maybe it was best that she understood why he'd left her. But if it was, then why did it have to hurt so much?

CHAPTER EIGHT

ANDREW threw his jacket on the passenger seat and backed away, slamming the door of the truck. "You ready to go?" he called out to Brody, who was just finishing off his coffee.

Brody lifted his mug for one last drink. "I'll put this inside," he said when it was empty. Andrew watched his friend stomp inside to deposit his cup. Brody had been more help than Andrew had expected. Anything Andrew needed Brody got it—or knew someone who could. Even today Brody had taken the day away from his own operation to go to Fort McLeod and the auction that was happening there. By the end of the day the three geldings already in residence would have new roommates.

Brody came back out of the house and shut the door behind him. "You tell Jen where we're going today?"

"Why would I do that?" Andrew checked the hitch one last time and straightened, regarding Brody curiously. Brody opened his own truck door, but leaned against it for a few moments.

"Just thought after the dance and all…"

God, Jen had been right. The more Andrew thought about it, the more he realized that whatever was between them, whatever he had to work through, it had been a mistake to try to fix it in front of the eyes of Larch Valley. First Agnes, then Clay, and now Brody.

"Did Lucy put you up to this?"

Brody shrugged, got in his truck and rolled down the window. "She and Jen are good friends," he admitted. "But I've known both of you a lot longer, bro."

Andrew climbed into his own cab and hit a button, rolling down the passenger window, determined not to let his friend know how much his words troubled him. "Hey, Dear Abby, let's shelve the advice for the lovelorn and get on the road." Brody's answering laugh made him grin. "I'll see you at the Fort," Andrew called out, rolling the window up and hitting the power button on the stereo deck.

They pulled out of Lazy L, Andrew in front, Brody in the rear.

It was a good day for driving. A bit cool, but clear, with a sharp wind coming from the west that promised milder hours ahead. Andrew reached over and changed the satellite station. He turned up the volume, feeling the bass while the gravely voice of Chad Kroeger filled the cab.

Yes, a good day for driving. A good day for clearing minds. He was still trying to wrap his head around what Jen had told him about Gerald. How could it be that their memories of him were so drastically different? Who was right? Or did the answer lie somewhere in the middle?

At the junction he turned north, with the plan of going past Larch Valley and across to Claresholm before turning south again. He hadn't driven this route in years, and he looked forward to it today. The spring grass was greening up, the sky was an endless blue, and for once the stress that seemed to settle in his shoulder blades was gone.

He checked his side mirror, saw Brody tapping a rhythm on his steering wheel and smiled. The exit for Larch Valley appeared on his left, the old service station long forgotten as the sign for the new one heralded high above the trees. He braked gently as he came upon a transport hauling livestock.

A peek through the slats told him the trailer was full of horses. His brow furrowed. Going to the same auction they were? Or straight to the slaughterhouse? Traveling this road, he wondered if they were horses being sent up from the States. Now that horse slaughter was banned south of the border, more and more animals were being sent north.

He sighed, taking a look at the road into town, knowing that on Main Avenue the morning was getting underway. What was Jen doing today? Baking, naturally. He could picture her there, behind her counter, wearing her plain white apron, her hair up in the perky tail she wore when working, smiling at her customers.

But she didn't smile at him these days. Since the dance she'd stayed as far away as possible. Not that he blamed her. He'd expected it to happen after he'd told her the truth. And now that they'd cleared the air—well, most of it anyway—he didn't know what to believe. He'd tried for years to get any sort of approval from Gerald, so that he would understand why Andrew had made the choice to be a veterinarian. To make Gerald see he wasn't a waste. To make him proud. According to Jen, Gerald had been all those things. Why, then, had he never showed Andrew?

He turned the radio down slightly, wiping a hand over his chin. He hadn't realized how much his leaving had hurt her the first time, and the last thing he wanted to do was hurt her again. He cared about her too much.

As that thought pulsed through his brain, he saw the trailer ahead of him shift and his stomach took an uneasy roll. Something wasn't right. He slowed down, giving the driver room to straighten himself out. But suddenly the load shifted again and the entire truck crossed the center line. The cab shifted back to the right, sharply. Too sharply.

"God, he's gonna go!" Andrew shouted it to the empty

truck. It happened in an instant, even as it seemed to play out in slow motion: the sharp jerk, the dust swirling up off the shoulder, the trailer tipping, tipping…

Heart in his throat, Andrew slammed on the brakes and felt his own empty trailer sway behind him.

Jen put the last row of lemon cookies in the display case, already thinking of the chocolate cakes she had to ice for the lunchtime crowd. The café expansion was paying off; her menu was small, but varied each day, and she couldn't deny that catering Andrew's benefit had been a boon. More than one person had come in saying they'd been there and had her beef on a bun or her hummus dip. Suzanne came each day after school and worked the smaller supper crowd, but until then Jen was alone. It meant she was getting up at four a.m. each day to start the necessary baking of bread and sweets, in addition to making a different soup each day. There wasn't time left after opening to do much baking.

She was starting to face the fact that she was going to have to hire extra help—an added expense but a necessary one. She slid the glass case door shut and sighed. She couldn't keep this pace up forever. In addition to the day's baking, at mid-morning she filled huge baking pans with some sort of hot entrée: lasagna, creamy chicken pasta, shepherd's pie. It was good home cooking and country baking her patrons asked for, and that was what they got.

But she was tired.

She couldn't get Andrew off her mind, not even when she was trying to sleep during the few precious hours she wasn't at Snickerdoodles. She turned what he'd said over and over in her mind, trying to puzzle it out. It had been over two weeks since she'd seen him, and they'd both said things… well, they'd said things that needed saying. She couldn't believe Gerald wasn't his father. If not Gerald, who? She stirred cocoa into icing sugar and butter, frowning. This was precisely what Andrew—and Gerald, for that matter—wouldn't want. Speculation and gossip. No one would ever hear his secret from her.

When the cakes were frosted, she went to the window and turned over the "Open" sign. She opened the inside door and put in the door stop, letting the scent of her bread announce the time, just as she'd done when Snickerdoodles had simply been a bakery. Now the smell of fresh-baked bread was joined by that of warm muffins and fragrant coffee. She'd get the coffee-breakers next, as she was building the day's entrée of baked penne pasta with Italian sausage.

Her first coffee break customer was Agnes Dodds, who had begun delaying opening her shop until nine-fifteen each morning. She briskly made her way into the bakery each day with an insulated mug that announced "I'm not old, I'm experienced" and bought a fresh brewed coffee and a cranberry muffin.

"Good morning, Mrs. Dodds." No matter how old Jen got, she couldn't quite seem to call her Agnes. It didn't match with the strict, shrewd teacher she'd once known.

"Why, good morning, Jennifer." Agnes didn't believe in shortening names either. She filled her cup from the urn, gave a satisfied sniff of the brew before putting on the cover, and marched to the cash register.

"Cranberry muffin?"

"It is Friday. I'm feeling adventurous."

Jen's lips twitched. "Then might I suggest banana nut?"

"Just the thing."

Jen tucked it into a small paper bag and rang in the sale.

"How is that young Laramie boy doing? I heard he's quite set up now, and even has a few new residents."

"I…I don't know." The mention of Andrew's name sent a fluttery feeling over her, and she looked down at the keys of the register before looking up again.

"Oh, come now. No sense playing coy, Jennifer." Agnes's eyes were shrewd as she smiled. "Everyone saw that kiss. It's about time he came to his senses. I always thought you two made a fine pair."

Jen gritted her teeth. "We're not a couple, Mrs. Dodds. It was just a kiss."

But Agnes wasn't deterred. "Oh, don't worry, dear," she said, reaching over and giving her hand a pat. "He'll come around."

Jen's hand shot across the counter, holding out Agnes's change as the bell above the door rang and her friend Lily Germaine came in. "Have a good weekend, Mrs. Dodds."

As Agnes's quick step took her to the door, Jen sighed and looked up into Lily's amused face.

"Don't you start," Jen warned. She brushed her hands on her apron. "Did you come in to buy something or just to pester?"

Lily's pretty blue eyes sparkled. "We are in a tizzy, aren't we?"

"That's been happening all week. The prodding, not the tizzy," she added as Lily's grin widened. "Do you know I spent a lot of money and elbow grease renovating this place, but nine times out of ten the people that come in don't comment on the changes, they mention Andrew?"

"Jealous? That Lazy L is getting more attention than you?"

Jen huffed and went to the back, returning with two apple pies she'd decided to make that morning. She opened the display door and put them in, while Lily came behind the counter and opened another door, closing it again with a cookie in hand.

"Not jealous," Jen replied. "I want Drew's project to be a success." More than just his project. She wanted good things for him. She looked up at Lily. Her friend had missed the dance, but Jen had been certain to fill her in on the details over therapeutic glasses of merlot and double chocolate brownies. She hadn't filled her in on the rest. "But it's not the rescue ranch that's causing the buzz. It's that stupid kiss."

She broke open a roll of dimes, emptying them in the till drawer, feeling slightly helpless and relieved that it was only Lily in the shop at the moment. "It took me a long time to get over him the first time. I spent a lot of energy building this business and my own life. And suddenly the most important thing I've done lately is kiss a guy at a dance. It's frustrating."

"Jen, you kissed him. You didn't marry him and change your name or anything."

Lily bit into her cookie and tossed her dark hair over her shoulder. At twenty-seven, she was the best friend Jen had in Larch Valley. She taught home economics at the nearby high school and barely looked older than her students.

"In this town, kissing him in public is just about the same thing."

Lily laughed. "That's why I don't date cowboys."

Jen couldn't help it. She chuckled too. "You're good for me, Lily."

"Well, at least I'm good for something."

"Why aren't you at school?"

Lily's eyes twinkled again. "Professional Day. I have to be there, but not for sessions. I'm going in to reorganize the sewing patterns or something." She polished off the cookie and grabbed a napkin to wipe her hands. "Speaking of sewing, how'd your cowboy like the curtains?"

"He's a man. He didn't say anything, or take them down, so I figure they met with his approval. Thank you for doing them. And for putting together the fingertip towels."

"Anytime. The windows here would look fantastic with café rods and panels. I have some great material that would match."

The door opened once more and Jen nodded. "I trust your judgment, you know that. And I'd be glad of the help."

"You got it. I've got a couple of girls who could use some extra credit time. Hemming curtains would be just the thing." Lily sent a sly wink and a smile.

"Miss O'Keefe?"

The voice that said her name was bursting with urgency. Jen looked over at Mark Squires, the manager who had signed off on her loan. His tie was crooked, and it looked as if he'd run his hands through his hair several times.

"My gosh, what is it?" She scurried around the counter while Lily shut the screen door that had been left gaping open.

"I just came down the highway to work. There's been an accident at the junction into town. Your man…"

Her heart plunged. "Is Andrew okay? Was he hurt?"

"No, no, he's fine. It's the horses…"

Mark's face paled as he took a few deep breaths. "A tractor trailer overturned. It was full of stock. Laramie's there, as well as Hamilton's men. I just thought you'd want to know."

"Of course. There must be something we can do to help without getting in the way. Are the RCMP there yet?"

"They're directing traffic."

Jen went to the coffee dispenser and filled a large cup. "Here," she said, holding it out. "You look like you could use this."

"Thanks, Jen." He checked his watch. "I'm already late, but I thought you'd want to know, considering…"

Yes, yes, considering. The whole town expected it now, but under the circumstances Jen ceased to care.

"Thank you for telling me, Mr. Squires," she replied, trying to keep her voice calm. She was still shaking from the momentary thought that Andrew had been hurt. She saw him to the door and turned back to face her friend.

"What are you doing?" Lily laid a hand on her arm.

Jen knew what she wanted, and she didn't care if it made sense or not. She wanted to be with Andrew. She could already picture him there, working on the side of the road—dear God, a whole trailer full of horses. The past didn't matter. She wanted to support him now.

"You won't be able to get through to the school until they open that road, Lily."

"Jen…"

"I've got to go to him, Lily. If you knew—" Her voice broke off, catching as she thought of not only their last conversation but the reason why he'd chosen this line of work in the first place.

"What I know is he left you and broke your heart, and here you are running after him again." Lily's brow furrowed with disapproval. "Jen, think about it for one minute. Don't be stupid."

But Jen shook her head. "I have thought about it." She went to Lily and gripped her fingers. "I know him better than anyone. I knew his father too, and… Oh, Lily, I'm not at liberty to tell you about it. Believe me, I know he hurt me. It is not something a heart forgets."

But her voice softened as she remembered how he'd looked, sounded as he'd told her about Gerald. She had given him space because that was what she thought he needed. But not today.

"I know why he left now, and I have to help him. My eyes are wide open, Lil. I know what I'm getting into. I will not leave him when he needs me."

Lily's eyes had filled with tears. "It's your choice," she whispered hoarsely. "You're a big girl and can make your own decisions. Just tell me what I can do to help."

Jen cleared her throat and took a deep breath. "Can you man the cash register? There won't be any lunch today, but if you could keep the bakery part open…"

"Consider it done."

Jen took a box of gloves and shoved them in a bag. "I've got my cell. Call if there's trouble and I'll do the same."

She didn't know what she could possibly do to help, but she remembered Andrew's face the day he'd told her about putting down that colt. The scene on the highway would be awful. She didn't want him to go through it alone.

By the time Jen reached the scene, the fire department was cutting through the top of the trailer. She swallowed as she saw the blood on the road; the men with grim faces trying to help as best they could. For a moment all she could do was stare at the chaos before her.

Everyone with a spare pair of hands in Larch Valley was now working to free the horses from the twisted wreckage of the trailer. Jen looked to her left; a man was sitting by the side of the road, looking dazed and stunned. The local RCMP detachment's vehicles were parked on either side of Highway 22, barring traffic. Jen craned her neck but couldn't see Andrew anywhere. She approached the closest officer, who was at the moment directing a tow truck to the front of the line.

"Grant?"

Constable Grant Simms turned his head at the sound of her voice. She would remember his face as long as she lived—drawn, tired, and clearly distressed. She put her hand on his arm. "Grant? Am I okay parked at the old service station? I'll move if I'm not."

She'd parked there because it was abandoned and off the side of the road, out of the way. "We don't need rubberneckers, Miss O'Keefe."

"I came to help."

After a slight pause, he relented. "Yes, your car's okay,"

he agreed, looking toward her car and nodding. "Nothing coming through here anyway."

"Have you seen Andrew Laramie?"

Simms sent an annoyed look over his shoulder. "He and Hamilton were setting up a temporary corral last I saw."

The flashing lights on the cruisers were meant to warn away traffic, but Jen knew the highway would be closed at either end anyway. Right now, the air was filled with the squeals of panicked, injured horses and the shouts of men.

She watched, horrified, as two of the firemen cut open another compartment, releasing the horse inside. Tears stung the back of her eyes as she saw the animal try to rise. The men backed away from the flailing hooves, until one man came forward, fearless, skillfully moving so his body could guide the mare to the side of the road, where a portable pen had been set up. Andrew.

Jen watched, fascinated, as Andrew used only the presence of his body and movement to get the terrified horse to go where he wanted it to go. His dark blond head disappeared and reappeared again. Brody Hamilton was leading another horse through the makeshift gate. The scene seemed to take on more order as she saw groups working together.

She saw Andrew pause, lean over and place his hands on his knees, catching his breath. He looked so tired, so…worn. She took a pair of latex gloves from the box she'd brought, dropping the remainder on the hood of a nearby car. They weren't surgical quality, but beggars couldn't be choosers. She strode across the highway to Andrew, while the sounds and smells of suffering assaulted her from every direction.

When he looked up and saw her coming his shoulders relaxed and his eyes filled with gratitude—and something stronger. She wiggled her fingers into the gloves and went to his side. "What do you want me to do? I'm here to help."

"Jen." It sounded strangely like a benediction. He reached out and roughly grabbed her, pulling her close in a brief but tight hug. She rubbed his back, realizing just how awful this must be for him. He was in the business of saving animals, and anyone with two eyes could see that not every horse would be saved today. She held on while his fingers dug into her back.

"Hey, Doc!" A shout came from behind them, and she stepped out of his arms to see one of the Prairie Rose ranch hands waving at them. Andrew put a hand on her arm. "This isn't pretty. Be sure."

"What do you need?" she insisted, feeling misgiving swirling in her stomach but determined to see it through. There was suffering going on here, and she wanted to help.

"My bag's beside my truck. If you'll run to get it…"

"I'll meet you over by Hal," she responded, setting off for his half-ton at a trot.

When she turned the corner to where Hal had indicated, she watched, fascinated, as Andrew went to the side of a beautiful bay stallion which was struggling to get up and failing abysmally. The horse dropped to its side, and she hustled over as Andrew looked up.

"What is it?" she asked, giving the wounded animal a respectable berth and handing him the bag.

"Broken radius, both sides," he replied, his eyes never leaving the animal. "He has to have hit something straight across. A metal bar, maybe. The fractures are identical, right across here." Andrew motioned with his hand where the injuries were. He withdrew a syringe from the bag and measured out medication.

As Jen watched, he knelt by the animal, his hands patting the heaving neck. His fingers were gentle, soothing and yet capable, and for a flash she remembered how they'd felt holding her hand as they'd danced during the waltz. They were hands that knew how to heal.

"I'm sorry, old boy," he murmured, administering the needle. Moments later the horse stopped struggling and a second needle was produced. Jen's eyes blurred with tears as the horse stilled completely, Drew hung his head and gave the neck a pat. "It's better than having him suffer," he said quietly, and rose from his knees. She wiped her fingers beneath her eyes as she saw the slump of his shoulders.

And when Andrew lifted his head and looked right at her, his face etched with resignation and acceptance, her heart threatened to beat clear out of her chest.

His face was dirty, his hands streaked with mud and blood. His lips were a grim line as he paused for the shortest of moments, eyes fixed on her. He looked exhausted, and angry, and unreachable. There were so many complications in their way…choices she refused to make…but none of it mattered to her heart. Like the initials carved into the bench in the town square: JO + AL. It was just as true today as it had been then. She couldn't have stopped the feelings any more than she could have stopped this morning's accident. Both were forces out of her control.

A shout echoed and he looked away, reaching down for his bag and moving on. Jen made her feet move, following him. Feeling it was one thing. Letting him know was another. And it was better he didn't know. Lily's words echoed in her head: *don't be stupid.* And her response that her eyes were wide open. She meant it. Wanting to be there for him, caring for him and supporting him, that was one thing. Letting herself be vulnerable to him was another. She knew the difference.

Andrew turned a corner and disappeared, but for some reason Jen turned her head to the right. There, in the tall grass beyond the shoulder of the road, was a roan mare. She was lying on her side, but something told Jen she wasn't injured. She scrambled down the bank and went to the mare's side.

"Hello, beautiful girl. Oh, look at you." There was a small cut on the neck, but otherwise she seemed fine. Jen stripped off her gloves and reached out, rubbing her nose, crooning soft words. The dark eyes looked into hers, and then with one fast movement, the mare was up and staring at her through a shaggy forelock.

"Stay here. I'll be right back."

Jen climbed back up the slight shoulder and found Hal again. "Hey, Hal, you got a halter in there somewhere?"

"Sure." Hal must have assumed she was on Andrew's errand, because he handed it to her and said, "Tell Laramie there's room for two more in our trailer and one more in his."

She took the halter and went back down to where the horse waited. She was a calm, sweet thing, and Jen cautiously approached, knowing she could still be spooked so easily in the chaos.

"Hello, again." She kept talking in a low voice. "I'm going to assume you're halter-broke, pretty girl. Yes, that's it." She slid the halter over the nose and behind the ears. "Now, will you come with me? I hear there's room in a truck for you."

She gave a tug on the halter, but the mare didn't move.

Jen heard a frantic whinny from the highway and blinked. She didn't know what had caused the accident but the aftermath was horrible. How had Andrew been so close? Where had he been going? The questions came to the fore now that the rest had sunk in. All she knew was that these animals were extremely fortunate he had been close by.

She laid her face against the mare's neck. "I know, it's frightening. But I'm here to help you, beautiful." She stroked the smooth hide. "Come, now, there's a girl."

She gave another slight tug and this time the mare followed, across the brown grass, up the embankment, to the shoulder of the road next to the Lazy L trailer.

CHAPTER NINE

ANDREW looked up and saw Jen leading a roan mare by the halter, her ponytail swinging behind her and the dirtied white apron looking out of place. His mouth dropped open as he both admired her willingness to help and despaired of her lack of judgment. She was a baker, not a rancher. It was clear to him that the mare was pregnant. He should have examined her before Jen had done anything. Besides, didn't she know that an animal of that size could hurt her if startled or injured? The last thing he wanted was Jen hurt. He'd do anything to make sure that didn't happen.

He set his jaw and strode over to where they were standing, just outside his trailer. "What are you doing?"

"Bringing you Lazy L's latest resident." She looked up at him and smiled. The warmth of it hit him in the gut, sending warning bells pealing.

"Dammit, Jen, these animals could be injured! Unpredictable! You might have been hurt."

"I'm fine," she responded calmly, but the expression of accomplishment faded from her face. Momentarily he felt small and petty, but he knew the danger was real. And he wouldn't see her hurt for the world.

She kept a firm hold on the mare's halter. "Hal said you

have room for one more. She has a cut on her neck, but otherwise looks fine."

"Except that she's with foal." He bit the words out, hearing the sharp tone and yet unable to stop it. Maybe it was a delayed reaction to the accident. Maybe it was because he recognized his own weakness and fear and hated it.

Andrew watched the slow realization cross her face as his words sank in. Her fingers clutched the halter as if suddenly more protective, and her wide-eyed gaze strayed to the mare's belly. "She is?"

He nodded. He was so tired, with so many feelings running through him today he couldn't even think of categorizing them. His one thought as his own vehicle had threatened to jackknife had been of her. Just her. So much that when he'd seen her he'd wanted nothing more than to bury his face in her sweet-smelling hair and hold on. But below it all was a simmering anger so complicated he had to work very hard at keeping it there rather than bubbling out. It didn't all have to do with Jen, and he didn't want to lash out more than he had to just because she was there. It wasn't fair to either of them.

The plain truth was none of these horses should be here. He'd been tempted to have a go at the driver of the truck until the RCMP constable had stepped in, and he'd focused instead on the animals that were suffering. He realized it was lucky that he and Brody had been starting out for Fort McLeod with empty trailers and had happened along when they had. But it could have been him on that road, injured, and who would care?

He didn't like the answer that immediately popped into his head. Oh, he'd done a fine job of pushing away the people he cared about while he was pursuing his career. Including the woman in front of him.

"Let me load her up." He stopped snapping, knowing Jen was only trying to help. He tried to put the smile back on her face, feeling guilty for erasing it in the first place. "We're almost done here. I've got to get these animals settled."

"All of them?" She looked around. Brody's trailer was holding four and the mare would make four in Andrew's.

"More than this. Some are dead. They'll be disposed of. Others are injured and need care. I'm not set up for surgery. Doc Watts in Pincher Creek is looking after those cases." He gestured toward the portable corral set up on the east side of the road. He'd planned on coming back from Fort McLeod with maybe half a dozen horses. Not three times that.

"I can take the easier cases and the mare will need an ultrasound. Brody and I'll be making another trip each. That gives me sixteen head. There's twenty one that need putting up. He's taking the other five, and he'll foster them there until we decide what happens next."

Her mouth dropped open. He took the halter from her hand and gently urged the mare up inside the trailer and secured her.

When he came back, Jen had removed her bloody and dirty apron and was twisting it in her hands. Her hair had been ripped from her ponytail by the wind and exertion, and strands blew across her face in the morning breeze. His curt responses had done their work. The tender glances they'd shared minutes before were gone. He'd been cold and dismissive. The way he'd effectively taken her joy away just now…he hated himself for it.

The truth was, being with Jen was sometimes the one thing that didn't hurt these days. And he'd driven her away. In the two weeks since the dance she hadn't spoken to him. Not once. Not until today.

And then she'd come running to him, and he hadn't been able to stop the hope that had pulsed through him at the sight of her. Why had she come?

"How did it happen, Drew?"

At her soft question he started. For a split second it seemed she was reading his thoughts and asking how they had reached this point. *Well, I found out I wasn't a Laramie*, he thought, with more than a hint of bitterness. But then he realized she was asking about the accident.

"I don't know. The driver said a wind gust, but I doubt it. I was right behind him and I didn't feel a thing. He seems pretty young. I'm sure we'll hear more about it later. It's better to let the cops sort it out."

"All those animals…dead," she lamented, her voice breaking a little on the last word. She gestured with an arm at the scene which finally bore some semblance of order.

"They would have been dead tomorrow anyway," he answered coldly. When there was an accident everyone came out in force, but who was there in the abattoir? No one. "Every one of these horses was on its way to the slaughterhouse."

Jen reached out and put a hand on his forearm. He tried to ignore the warmth it provided.

"What will happen to them now?"

"I'll figure it out. They won't be going there, I can promise you that. I won't let that happen."

He lifted weary eyes to hers. There were too many details to attend to right now, and he wasn't exactly good company. The truth was, it was a good thing the Mounties had shown up. His fuse was particularly short, and he knew damn well there'd been no wind. He'd rushed to the cab of the transport and yanked the driver out. Brody had pulled him away and told the driver to call it in while they began getting the horses out.

"What can I do to help you?" The hand on his arm squeezed, and he felt her gentle reassurance tugging at him. The adrenaline was wearing off and he had a full day's work ahead and then some. It would be too easy to pull her into his arms and drink in the comfort he knew she was offering. But wouldn't she consider that taking advantage too? Like she had at the dance? No, it was better if they left things the way they were. He needed to focus on Lazy L.

"You've already helped. Thank you for coming, but you should go back to the bakery."

He could tell he had offended her as her chin flattened. "I'm in your way," she said.

"Of course not." But in a way she was. Having to euthanize the horses had meant reliving the day he'd made his decision and he hated it. It made him feel raw and helpless and he'd rather Jen not witness any more of it. She'd seen him as weak as he ever cared to be. She had a way of making him feel vulnerable. Arranging to transport the bodies wasn't something he wanted her to see, either.

"Yes, I am," she insisted. "But will you let me know if there's anything I can do?"

"Yeah, sure."

His cool tone did its work. Jen stepped back. "I'll see you around," she said, turning her back on him and striding toward where she was parked.

Jen traveled up the long dirt lane for the first time since the dance, with the scent of supper filling the interior of the car. She'd returned to Snickerdoodles to find everything ticking along like a good watch. Lily had filled in like a champ, and Suzanne had come in after school. It seemed Jen wasn't needed anywhere. Andrew had made it very clear at the accident site that she was in the way. Perhaps she always had been. And with new recognition of her own feelings she wondered if he wasn't also in hers, constantly dragging her mind away from what she should be focusing on: her business.

But the feeling didn't last long. She'd really had no option than to go and offer her help. Now the nerves of the morning had started to die away and she felt exhaustion setting in. But who would give Andrew a break? His long day was just beginning. She'd kept picturing his face as he'd seen her walking across the road. As if she were the answer to everything. She was afraid to be that answer. And yet she wanted to be with him. To help him. To see him smile at her again, the way he had as he'd asked her to dance at the benefit.

She parked next to a strange truck and shut off the ignition. Lucy's SUV was already parked in the shade of a poplar, and as Jen got out of her car Lucy came out of the house to stand on the verandah. It had only taken one hurried phone call to Lucy for Jen to understand how the day would play out. Brody, Andrew, and several other neighbors would be working to get the horses settled at Lazy L. And that many working men meant big appetites. Lucy had said she was planning on cooking something, but Jen had insisted. She had the ingredients she'd abandoned this morning and the baking was done. And Lucy was growing rounder by the day.

She waved at Lucy, who stood next to the railing with her hand on her belly. "Hey, Mama." She smiled, shutting the driver's side door and opening the back one.

"Hey, yourself. Need a hand?"

Lucy came down the steps, looking cute this afternoon, dressed in maternity jeans and a light flowered T-shirt that had a tiny white bow just beneath her breasts. It had only been a little over a year since their wedding, and already they were starting their family. A twinge of longing struck Jen's heart. It wasn't necessarily the baby, she realized. It was that her friend looked so perfectly, peacefully happy. Would she ever have that?

She thought back to her conversations with Drew. There would never be anything perfect or peaceful with them, whether she'd fallen for him or not. Maybe there was simply too much baggage they would never get past.

"I brought drinks," Lucy said as Jen held out a bag containing several dozen buns. "You wouldn't let me cook. I thought the least I could do was provide pop. And I brought my coffee-maker. We can make two pots at a time."

"Great idea." Jen reached in for the first box, containing the main course. She'd also packed bags of buns, three pies, and one of the chocolate cakes still left from the morning. "Any idea how they're making out?"

"They're getting there. We haven't been here that long. Brody brought Andrew's stock out here, but then he came home with our five and got them squared away. Clay and Dawson are here. And Tom Jr. brought out the feed he promised and stayed to help."

Jen followed Lucy inside and placed the box on the counter next to the sink. The room was neat as a pin, and cheerful with the gingham cloth still on the table and the curtains at the window. A dirty coffee cup sat in the sink and there were toast crumbs on the counter. It looked like a home. As she took the baking pan out of the box, still in towels, she frowned. Somehow, the more settled Andrew got, the more *un*settled she became.

Jen shook the thought away. "That makes five hungry men. And us. I hope it's enough."

They made another trip to the car, and Lucy unpacked the pies and cake while Jen heated the oven and put the pasta in to warm. This was a neighbor helping a neighbor. There was no reason why she should feel wifely simply because she'd cooked a meal and knew her way around his kitchen. The change in her feelings didn't mean *they* had changed. If anything, they were further apart than ever. He still didn't believe what she'd told him about Gerald. And she wasn't willing to trust her heart to a man who had no idea what he really wanted.

"I heard you went out to the scene," Lucy said conversationally, but Jen knew she was digging. Then again, there wasn't much to hide since the dance. Except the discovery that her old feelings weren't so old anymore.

"Lily watched the bakery."

Lucy laughed. "How is Lil? Do you know she showed up at the house with a whole crib set for the baby? Bumper pads, comforter, matching sheets. She claimed she had some leftover fabric."

Jen laughed. It sounded like Lily. "And you were thinking...leftover from what?"

"Exactly. What would *she* have baby material for?"

The women laughed. Lily made no secret of not being in a hurry for marriage *or* babies.

But Lucy was undeterred by Jen's attempt at diverting the topic. "Still...it's very telling that you went out there, don't you think?"

Jen's hands paused over the bun she was slicing. "I wanted to help. Isn't that what we do here in Larch Valley? Help each other?"

"And it had nothing to do with wondering if Andrew was okay?"

She paused, hiding her flushed cheeks as she put her back to Lucy, reaching for the butter. "Of course not. Mark Squires said Andrew and Brody were helping. I just went to lend a hand."

But she couldn't meet Lucy's eyes. Was this going to be the start of more gossip? Not from Lucy, of course. But there were lots of people helping today. How long would it take before it got around that she'd run to Andrew's side at the first opportunity? Probably only slightly longer than news of their kissing in public.

And she suddenly realized that their embrace today hadn't

been private either. Oh, what a tangled mess when emotions had to get involved!

Lucy's hand was gentle on Jen's shoulder. "Do you love him?"

Jen wheeled around, knitting her brows. She understood that Lucy was incandescently happy, and wanted others to be the same, but it wasn't that simple.

"I can't love him."

Lucy waved a hand at her. "Why ever not?"

But Jen knew she couldn't go into the reasons. They were all tied up with Gerald now, and it wasn't her story to tell. "It's complicated."

Lucy smiled, unconsciously rubbing her tummy. "Oh, isn't it always? And look. Here they come."

Through the screen door Jen saw five dusty men in jeans walking up from the barn, gesturing with their hands and talking. One—Jen recognized the dusty figure as Clay Gregory—said something that caused the rest of the group to laugh, and in the middle of it all was Andrew, carrying his hat in his hand, looking tired, but with an air of happy satisfaction about him.

He spied her car and hesitated, then turned his head sharply toward the house. The other men clumped on to the verandah ahead of him and made a show of removing their boots. Andrew came last, entering the kitchen in stockinged feet and shutting the screen door gently behind him.

Lucy'd herded the helpers down the hall to the bathroom, so they could wash up, which left Jen in the quiet kitchen with Andrew.

"I didn't expect to see you."

She blinked with surprise. "Am I in the way again?"

He had the grace to look uncomfortable. "I didn't mean it that way, Jen. I'm sorry for the way I spoke out at the accident scene. I didn't expect to see you back here after the way I acted."

His apology went a long way to mollifying her defensiveness, and her lips curved up in an easy smile. "You've been away from Larch Valley for a while, Andrew." She took the basket of buttered buns and placed it on the table. "I thought you might have figured it out at the benefit, but maybe not. We help each other here. Through thick and thin."

She stood back and folded her hands in front of her. He had to know a few sharp words weren't going to send her scurrying away for good. Heavens, she understood he was dealing with a lot. "I know how difficult it was for you today. And I knew you'd have extra manpower here. Bringing in food to help isn't a big deal. It's just my way of being your friend."

She minimized it to him, but refused to lie to herself. Yes, she probably would have helped in any case. But with Andrew it went deeper than that. It always would. If he ever needed her, no matter if he wanted it or not, she'd be there for him.

"People will talk. Aren't you worried about that?"

She looked down, slightly uncomfortable. Yes. She didn't like the gossip that tended to follow this sort of thing. Her coming here tonight would be taken as a statement of coupledom.

"I came to help in the best way I know how," she murmured. "That's all. I'm going to help, and I can't control what people say."

The men were returning to the kitchen and Jen greeted each with a smile and small talk, catching up with what was new. Unimportant details about who they'd seen at the grocery store, who'd been out to karaoke night the previous weekend. Did people not do this where he'd been? Despite longing for privacy, she knew she'd miss it if she left Larch Valley. She took a spoon and started scooping servings on to plates. Everyone here was connected, and there was comfort in it. Andrew remained quiet, only murmuring a thank-you when she handed him a plate.

Lucy fixed Brody's plate and handed it to him with a kiss, before going to the fridge for cans of pop. As she paused by the table his hand rested on her hip for a few moments. Jen swallowed against the lump in her throat. It was the kind of touch that said, *Hello, I'm here. Just here.* The kind of touch that said just as much as any words possibly could.

"Aren't you eating, Jen?" Tom Walker piped up from the table.

She forced a smile in response. "I don't know, Tom, did you boys leave anything?" she teased, but her heart wasn't in it. As the guys laughed, she added, "I'll get something later. Who wants coffee? Cake or pie?"

"Both!" came the answer from Dawson Briggs, and everyone laughed.

Jen found a chair for Lucy, and made her sit down with some coercing from Brody. It wasn't long before the men had finished eating. They lingered only a few minutes over coffee, and headed out the door with thanks for the meal. They had their own chores to do.

"I'll help clean up," Lucy insisted, but Jen shooed her away.

"No, you go home with Brody. If you're on your feet any longer he's going to fuss and flutter and drive you crazy. And he has your own stock to look after tonight."

Lucy looked at the pile of dishes and the sink—there was no dishwasher—and hesitated.

"Go," Jen insisted. "I'm going to have something to eat and these dishes won't take but a minute."

Lucy nodded, glancing out the door at Brody and Andrew, talking in the rosy light of sunset. "Talk to him, Jen."

"I don't seem to know what to say lately."

Lucy met her gaze evenly. "You know what? I thought that once too."

When the Hamiltons had gone, Jen filled the sink with

soapy water and started washing up. Andrew had disappeared to the barn again. Was he avoiding her? She scrubbed at a plate. Maybe, despite the few kisses they'd shared, he'd sensed her feelings went deeper than she had intended to show and it was his way of backing off.

But a simple thank-you would have been nice.

She had everything packed into one box and a light left on over the stove when she stopped. She was so proud of him for all he'd done today. He'd shown strength and compassion and ability in the way he'd taken charge of the situation. She knew Gerald would have been proud of him too. Maybe that was what Andrew needed to hear. Was it worth one more try?

CHAPTER TEN

OUTSIDE, Jen paused on the verandah, soaking up the evening. A mourning dove cooed a repetitive lonely call. The once empty barn echoed tonight with soft whickers and the stamping of hooves, instead of lying silent as it had for many months. Jen smiled a wistful smile, remembering when the ranch had been vital and alive, and pleased it would be so again. Even if it wasn't quite the same as before, this was what Lazy L needed. Purpose. The barn was meant to be full. The house was meant to be a home. It had lain fallow like the fields for too long. It was so sad that Gerald wasn't here to see it. To see his son where he'd always wanted him to be. Perhaps in time Lazy L would provide whatever it was Andrew was looking for.

A light shone through the window at one end—the one where Andrew had set up his medical area. Jen put the box down on the step and went toward the beacon.

Andrew sat at a plain desk, packing gauze and bandages into a steel box. She watched him for a moment in the shadows of the doorway. Despite their complications, he was a good man. Maybe that was why it was so difficult to let go. To realize their relationship would never be what she'd once hoped it would. Wondering if what they had was enough. Or too much.

"I'm taking off now."

He jumped at the sound of her voice, and then let out a breath. His gaze met hers, his unreadable. "I'm sorry, Jen. I meant to take a quick look at the stock after supper, but one of the geldings needed his dressing changed, and…"

He looked sincere, and Jen waved a hand. "It's all right, Andrew. I understand."

"Thank you for supper."

"You're welcome."

Silence drew out. He dipped his head and started rolling gauze again.

"Andrew?"

"Hmm?"

She paused, wishing he would look up, afraid of what would happen if he did. She was tired of fighting her feelings for him. She'd done a lot of self-talk lately, about all the reasons why she couldn't fall for him, but the truth was she had. Even when she knew it was a mistake. A part of her knew it was better if he stayed aloof. A bigger part wanted to feel the delicious jolt she knew would happen if their eyes met.

It would be a mistake to have him as a lover, but she wasn't sure she could bear to lose him altogether again.

"Do you think someday we could manage to be friends?"

That snapped his head up. He put down the gauze, rested his elbows on the table, propping his chin on his thumbs. "Do you? There's an awful lot of water under the bridge."

"So how are we going to manage?" She held her breath. How would they get by if every time they saw each other it was either to argue or gaze at each other longingly? It was no way to live. It wasn't how she wanted to live, she realized.

He gave the tiniest of shrugs. "We'll manage. People do. In time it'll get easier."

In time. Did that mean he was finding this as difficult as she was? The thought sent a strange turning through her chest. Why was it that the further apart they got, the more she wanted him? The more she tried to hold on?

Something had changed today, something vital and alive between them, in the moment he'd looked up and seen her crossing the asphalt. She was tired of running from it.

"I wish you'd had time to talk to Gerald," she began. His jaw tightened, but she plowed on, hoping to help him past some of the resentment he clung to so stubbornly. "Now that I know why you left, many of the things he said seem to fit. I know he regretted your estrangement. He would have been proud of you today."

"Jen, I spent a lot of years in a high-profile industry." He shut the box with a firm click of the latch. "And I learned that there are millions of ways to spin things. But this is one time that there is no spin. It just is what it is. I should never have come back. I realize that now."

Shock rippled through her at the casual yet firm way he said the words. And a glimmer of fear of losing him so quickly when they had hardly reconnected. "So you're leaving? Now?"

"Hardly." He picked up the box and stowed it neatly on a shelf behind him. "I've sunk money and energy into this place. This morning I had three horses under my care; tonight I have nineteen. Soon to be twenty." He faced her, hands on his hips. "I couldn't leave now if I wanted to."

"But you do want to?"

"I thought this would be starting over." Giving in, he tossed the pen down and leaned back in his chair. "I thought it would be one last chance to prove myself to him. But it's not starting over. It's more like reliving all the failures, and I should have seen it and didn't."

Jen's hope plummeted. Why couldn't he see the reasons he'd returned clearly, like she could?

"You have never been a failure! What would make you say such a thing?"

"You tell me." He watched her coolly, wondering how their impressions of Gerald could differ so utterly. "You tell me how I should feel, when I worked myself to the bone trying to show Gerald that I'd made a good choice. That I could make something of myself to—"

He broke off, swallowed against the sudden lump in his throat. "To be a son he could be proud of. And tell me what I should think when I never received a single letter in return."

She twisted her fingers. "I don't know, Drew. I swear. All I know is that when I saw him he talked about you. I wish I had some way to show you. To prove it."

"I don't know what I thought I'd accomplish by coming back here."

That hurt, because she knew that she'd factored very little in his decision to return. "Maybe you did it because there are loose ends that need tying up. Or a circle that needs completing. Things that need to be resolved." Their relationship was one of those things. He needed to make peace with himself since Gerald was no longer here. She took a step forward. "I think you were meant to come back."

"Well, it doesn't seem to be working so well."

"How can you say that? Look at what you've accomplished! You have brought Lazy L back to life. You have rallied the community around a cause. You have saved the lives of several animals already." She tried a smile, but it felt bittersweet. If only he'd done it sooner. She wondered if he'd made the same wish too. "I *know* Gerald is proud of you, wherever he is." She held other words on her tongue, about him changing her. About bringing her back to life as well as the ranch. She was afraid to say them. It would be revealing too great a weakness, and now, when he was talking about his coming back being a mistake, she knew she'd been right to keep her feelings to herself.

"Can we change the subject? There's been enough doom and gloom today." He offered a smile. "Would you like to see the mare?"

She would, and she accepted the diversion—for now. She usually didn't get silly over animals, but today, when the mare had looked into her eyes, Jen had fallen in love. "All right."

His chair scraped back and he went to move past her at the door. She didn't get out of the way quite fast enough and their bodies nearly brushed—close enough—she could feel him without actually making contact. She caught her breath and held it.

He'd been working all day in the dust and dirt, and suddenly the only thing she truly wanted was to touch him. Everywhere. Right here, in the wedge of light coming through the doorway, in the barn that was scented with horse and the sweet smell of fresh hay and the fragrance of the spring nighttime trickling through the open doors. To feel his arms around her and the beat of his heart against her cheek, like it had been at the dance. To leave all the heavy, mind-bending stuff behind them for a few blessed minutes.

For a moment her fingers stretched out, very nearly grazing the fabric of his T-shirt.

But he brushed by her and she let out the breath she'd been holding. He led the way down the corridor to a box stall. A velvety nose appeared and Jen smiled, delighted as the mare stuck out her head to be petted.

"Hello, beautiful. You're looking much better than you did this morning." The mare lifted her nose, leaning into Jen's hand as she scratched, and she laughed.

She turned to Andrew, who was standing a few feet behind her, his weight resting on one hip as he watched her with some amusement.

"What's so funny?"

"Not a thing." He stepped ahead so he was beside her and lifted his hand, scratching beneath the mare's mane. "You two get along like peas in a pod. She didn't take a liking to Clay at all."

"That's because Clay Gregory is a flirt." She rubbed the soft nose and crooned. "Isn't he, sweetheart? Good for you, giving him what for."

Andrew chuckled softly beside her.

"And don't let this one off the hook either," she murmured coyly to the mare. "He just pretends he's forgotten how to flirt."

"Hah!" came his ineffectual defense, and Jen laughed softly. For several seconds they petted the horse together.

"Is the foal all right?" The mare was so sweet, and Jen truly hoped there would be no further suffering after the accident.

"Yes, it's fine. I did an ultrasound late this afternoon, once she'd quieted."

"When's she due?"

"Best guess, seven to eight weeks."

"A summer baby."

His voice warmed. "It would seem so, yes."

She'd stopped petting, and the mare nuzzled again, looking for more attention. Jen rubbed between the horse's eyes. "Well now, beautiful. Considering how your day started, it seems you've found yourself in clover."

"Jen?"

Hope blossomed in her chest as he said her name softly and she closed her eyes. Maybe the mare had worked miracles, because the underlying tension from before seemed to have dissipated into the May breeze.

"I'm sorry, Jen. It's been a hard day."

She turned then and went to him. He wasn't avoiding her gaze anymore, and his hazel eyes were dark with sincerity. Before she could change her mind, she put out her hands and rested them on his ribs—not quite an embrace, but definitely crossing the line into physical contact. He felt warm and solid beneath her fingertips, and she could tell he was holding his breath.

But he stayed his ground, and she did the most natural thing in the world: she stepped forward and leaned against his chest, her arms forming a light embrace.

"I know it has," she murmured. "I didn't try to make it more difficult for you by bringing up your father."

"You didn't." His arms went around her too, holding her close. "You helped when I least expected it. Even when I sent you away."

"You must have known I would."

His breath was warm on her hair as she stilled, waiting for the answer.

"No," he whispered. "Not after I was so unbearable."

For several minutes they simply drew strength and comfort from each other.

She bit down on her lip. He was as receptive now as she'd ever seen him. Maybe this was her chance to reach him, to make him see exactly what he'd come home to instead of run away from.

"Can I say what I think? Will you listen? And then just think about it. Please?"

He hesitated, but finally agreed with a slight nod.

"Come here." She turned out of his arms, already missing the heat of his body against hers, but knowing there was no better time to make him see.

She led him to the end of the barn, where the sliding door remained open. She leaned against the heavy wood frame and looked out over the corral and fields beyond. Andrew stood in the middle of the doorway, his stance square, his hands in his pockets. She'd never seen a lonelier picture in her life. Tonight she saw what she had missed since his return. Not anger. Tonight she saw regret in him, and it broke her heart, because she knew he thought it was too late.

"This is yours, Andrew. Lazy L, despite what you think, is your birthright. Gerald knew it, and you knew it too, even as you rejected it for another path. I think you're horribly bound up in regret, and you didn't expect it to be this difficult coming home. I think you stopped hating Gerald a long time ago, because if you didn't care you wouldn't have tried so hard. But you're still hurting over it. And I think seeing me reminds you of that time with too much clarity. And so being with me probably makes you feel better and worse at the same time, and you don't know what to do with it."

She saw a muscle tick in his jaw. He refused to look at her, and instead she tried to see what he was seeing. Rolling hills of grass, black now in the growing darkness. Fences and the shadowed figures of horses beyond. Young ones, old ones, ones that were ill and others healthy. All horses he was trying to save.

And that was it, wasn't it? He was trying to save them all. To make up for what?

"You are doing a good thing here, Drew. And please don't interpret what I'm going to say as a criticism, but who are you really trying to save? The horses? Gerald? Your mother? Or is it yourself?"

She saw him swallow, and knew instinctively that she'd gone as far as she dared.

She moved from the door and half turned, facing his profile now. "There are some things, Drew, you are never going to be able to fix. But what you've got here is possibility.

Opportunity. Don't waste it by worrying about things that can't be changed. Just think about it, okay? That's all I ask."

She started to walk away but paused, knowing there was something else she needed to say. Something else he might need to hear. Her eyes stung as she let out a trembling breath. Their backs were to each other, but her voice resonated like ripples through the spring air.

"I still believe in you, Drew."

It was as close as she could get to admitting her true feelings and the urge to cry swooped in, fresh and brutal. And yet her feet refused to move. The reasons why she should go were still there, but they had somehow ceased mattering.

His choked reply sounded behind her. "Then you're a fool."

"No!" She spun then, rushing back to him, putting her hand on his arm. "Don't say that. You're a good man." She thought again of the haunted look in his eyes when they'd been working at the accident, his undisguised relief at seeing her and holding her close. "Everyone made mistakes, Drew. Me, you, Gerald, your mother. It's so easy to look back after the fact."

She took a step over, so that she was directly in front of him. She lifted her hand and put her fingers on his cheek. "I might hate that you left me all those years ago, but, Drew, you were eighteen. You did what you thought you had to. I might not like it, but I know you didn't do it to deliberately hurt me."

Drew closed his eyes, but behind them all he saw was the way she'd looked as he drove away that morning. Small and alone, and with the tracks of tears glimmering on her cheeks. Dammit, why was she being so generous? Couldn't she see her words were cutting him in half? And he didn't have the energy to fight her right now. Not tonight. Not after everything that had happened today.

He would rather die than hurt her again, and yet he needed her. She was the one person who knew the truth and she hadn't run away. Instead she was here. With tears in her eyes and her fingers on his skin.

He placed his palm over her hand and turned his head slightly, pressing a kiss on to the pad of her thumb. This morning he had come so close to losing her. Another few seconds either way and he would have been part of that accident. The trailer had started to go, and he'd nearly gone with it.

"Drew." She whispered his name and it reached inside of him and held. Everything else faded away, except her and the need rushing through him.

He reached out his right hand, commandeering the back of her neck, pulling her close as he kissed her. The sweet heat of her mouth was a surprise, and her fingers dropped from his cheek and instead dug into his biceps, holding on. He nipped her lip and heard her gasp against his mouth, prompting a satisfied smile. Renewed energy pulsed through his veins, bringing with it desire and hunger. His other arm pressed her close and lifted her so that her toes were off the floor, and he took the scattering of steps necessary to find a stall door. With the solid wood behind her, bolstering, she freed her hands and ran them through his hair. The sensation, coupled with the way she moaned into his mouth, only added to his greed.

She made him feel alive.

He wanted to scoop her up, take her inside the stall and lay her down on a blanket padded with fresh straw, with the sounds of the peepers for music and the glimmer of the moon and stars for light.

His mouth slid from her lips down to the hollow of her throat, where her heartbeat pulsed against him. It would be so easy, he thought. She was the one thing that hadn't changed, that made sense, that *still fit*.

"*Drew…*"

She whispered it, the syllable sliding through the air like silk.

He paused, and the doubt was enough to cool the passion roaring between them. He couldn't do this. As much as he wanted to, he couldn't.

And he did want to. Badly.

"What is it?" she said gently as he eased back from her. Her toes touched the floor once more. He could see the quick rise and fall of her breasts as she struggled for breath.

"We need to stop."

He watched as her face fell and the light went out of her eyes. And here he was, letting her down again. It seemed impossible that she could be upset. She'd been fighting him every step of the way. In the bakery. At the dance. But not this time.

She stood before him, her cheeks pale, eyes wide with what looked like disappointment. "Why?" he asked. "Why aren't you fighting me now? What's changed?"

She lifted her chin, while the corners of her mouth turned up wistfully. "We've both changed. Can't you see it?"

Something about her tone set him on edge. Not angry, but unsettled, uncomfortable, like when he put on a T-shirt that was just a bit too small.

"I'm not sure what you mean."

"The chip on your shoulder. It's gone. I'm not sure when it disappeared, but you're not so…defensive," she finished, as if searching for the right word. "Hurting, yes. But angry, not so much. And neither am I. I hadn't forgiven you, you see."

He knew exactly when that chip had taken a hike. It had been this morning, when he'd hit the brakes. Administering medicine to wounded horses, seeing death and destruction, had driven it even further away, and it had disappeared over the horizon the moment he'd seen her coming toward him. Even as he knew she deserved better, even as he knew he had so little to offer, she was the puzzle piece that had been missing. He hadn't expected forgiveness. The fact that she offered it to him was an unexpected gift.

"I was very nearly a part of that accident." He sighed, and shifted so they were both leaning with their backs against the door. He could feel her eyes on his face when she turned her head to look up at him. All evening his mind had played those few seconds over and over. All evening the feeling associated with the memory was exactly the same. A life of missed opportunities and regrets.

"I thought you just happened by."

"No, it was right in front of me. Something wasn't right, and then it was happening, and all over before I could barely take a breath. I stopped, and Brody stopped, and we went into function mode."

"Oh, Andrew. It must have been so difficult for you. I know how much you're dedicated to saving lives." She leaned her head back against the faded wood, looking up with sympathy.

She thought it was about the horses.

He gave a little laugh of irony, the chuckle catching on the lump in his throat.

"I'm so tired of having to prove myself and coming up short," he sighed. His gaze held hers, caught in the smoky depths that had always been able to see more than he liked. "It's exhausting. But I have no idea where to go from here. Kissing you solves none of it. And it's not fair to you. I can't give you what you want from me, Jen. You'd be better off getting in your car and going home."

"Is that what you want?"

He turned his head so that he was facing her, like two heads on a pillow. "No."

"What do you want?"

That was the million-dollar question—and one he had no answer to.

"I can only see today. But I know you, Jen, and I know you won't be happy unless you have everything. And I just don't have everything to give. I don't know if I ever will."

"Did I ask for that?"

"Yes."

Her back came away from the stall. "I did?"

"Yes." He, too, stepped away from the wooden barrier behind him. He reached for her and cupped her cheek. "Every time you kissed me in twelfth grade you wanted it all. The day I said goodbye it threatened to pull me in. And when I came back every time I looked in your eyes I knew you were a woman who would settle for nothing less than what you deserved. But that's not me, Jen. I'm not strong enough to let you go completely. And that's unfair to you."

"Why don't you let me decide that?"

He was so surprised at her question that he fell silent for the space of two beats, his lips dropping open. "Jen, I'm not ready for what you want. I don't know if I ever will be." The last thing he needed was to repeat the mistakes of the past. He refused to let Jen be a casualty of that again.

But she persisted, and her tenacity chipped away at the chinks in his resolve. "So don't be ready. Let's just take it bit by bit. Even if it means simply admitting that we're not as over as we thought we were. Being friends to each other. And going a day at a time."

It sounded good. It sounded almost too good. In a place where loneliness abounded and friendship seemed in short supply it was an offer he couldn't refuse. The idea of living in the moment felt liberating. When was the last time he'd done that?

"A day at a time I can do." He tried a smile, found it more ready than he'd expected. He pulled her close, letting his hands rest on the hollow of her back, his fingers trailing along her tailbone. He dipped his head and tasted her lips again, then a third time, longer, deeper.

"This day doesn't have to end yet." He knew what he was suggesting. He wanted her with him longer.

"Mmm," she replied lazily. "But if I stay…"

The thought hung in the air, and he finished the sentence in his mind. He had no doubt that she'd done the same.

"If you stay…"

She blinked, sighed, and took a small step back. Physically she'd barely moved half a dozen inches, but he felt the distance between them just the same.

"That might be best saved for another day. I'm not sure I'm ready for that yet."

He accepted it. This morning he'd snapped at her, and now they'd just somehow managed to forge a new peace. They'd started something…not quite a relationship, but something. All of that and sex added in probably wasn't the wisest choice.

And, if anything, he felt that he needed to make careful choices with Jen. What they had now was precious, tenuous at best. One day at a time.

"Then why don't I walk you to your car?"

"I'd like that."

He took her hand in his, the simple gesture touching him in unexpected ways. Together they left the barn, flicking out lights as they went, until they stood beside her car.

He opened her door, but as she went to get in he tugged her back.

"Will you come out again soon?"

She smiled softly as the moon went under a cloud, creating shadows on her face.

"Of course." She smiled again. "I'll want to check on the mare, now, won't I?"

"Just the mare?"

"Oh, there might be one or two more that I could spare some attention."

Her teasing smile lit all the dark places in his heart. If he wasn't careful he was going to fall headfirst in love with her again.

One day at a time.

"Drive carefully."

He watched until her car made the turn from the lane to the main road, the sound on gravel inordinately loud in the clear evening.

CHAPTER ELEVEN

"SHE'S doing well, don't you think?"

Jen leaned her elbows on the edge of the fence, watching the mare—now officially christened Beautiful—snip at pieces of lush grass. It was a Sunday, Snickerdoodles was closed, and she'd refused to play the "should I or shouldn't I?" game when it came to Drew and Lazy L. She had a need to feel the air on her face and she wanted to check on the mare. They had said one day at a time. What better day could they have than this?

"She's doing great. So are most of the others." Andrew leaned against the railing beside her, lazily shredding a thick blade of grass with his fingers. "Pokey's still on antibiotics, and a couple are skittish, but on the whole they've settled in."

"And have you settled in?" She was sure he hadn't meant to build his herd quite this quickly. But the question wasn't quite as intrusive as it would have been a week ago. There'd been a change in him—subtle, but noticeable. He was growing into his role at Lazy L and it showed.

"I'm getting there." His fingers finished the last strand of grass and it fluttered to the ground. "I'm glad you came out today."

"Me too."

He turned, putting his back to the horses in the pasture and leaning on the fence, hooking one heel over the other.

His hat shaded his eyes in the spring sunlight, the denim jacket over his wide shoulders warding off the chill of the unseasonably cool day. He looked irresistible, standing there, and on impulse Jen stood on tiptoe and touched a quick kiss to his lips.

"What was that for?" He raised an eyebrow, seemingly unperturbed, but with a twinkle lighting his eye.

"Do I need a reason?"

Andrew laughed then, a solid, warm, feel-good laugh that filled her to her toes. Right now she didn't need to probe into what the future held. They could just exist in today and know it was okay. Jen wanted to leave the worries of the business and the spectre of the past behind them.

But his laugh drifted away on the breeze and his eyes softened to a troubled golden color. "I wanted to do something today, and I didn't have the courage. But now you're here maybe..." He paused. "That sounds stupid, doesn't it?"

"What do you want to do?"

"Go through Gerald's things. I haven't yet. Haven't even gone into his room. And it's time. Someone should go through his clothing. I'm sure the goodwill could use it. Leaving it as it is feels wrong."

Jen smiled softly. It was a huge step for him, and one she was glad to see happen. "Of course I'll help you." She placed a hand against his chest and looked up into his face, understanding that he felt a little foolish asking. "No one should have to go through a parent's things alone."

They went inside. The house was so quiet it was disturbing, like walking through a church sanctuary. Andrew gave her hand a squeeze. "Why don't you go up? I'll grab a box for the clothing."

When Drew reached the top of the stairs, he took a breath. He had gotten as close as opening the door and standing on the threshold once, but that was all. He stepped forward now, relieved to see Jen inside the room. Her mere presence took away some of his anxiety.

He put the box at the foot of the bed. "Where do we start?"

They began with the dresser, taking out clothes and folding them into the bottom of the box. Drew tried not to think of the last time he'd seen Gerald wearing a certain shirt, or the several pairs of knitted wool socks his father had insisted upon wearing in the winter, but he couldn't escape the memories completely. Of the gruff working man who had been on the opposite side of arguments more times than Andrew could count.

"Oh, Drew, look." Jen pulled a tiny framed picture out from between two plain white undershirts. "You were so small. Look at the blond hair! And there is your mother."

He took the snapshot from her fingers, swallowing hard. It was a picture of the four of them: Gerald, Julie, Noah and himself. Everyone was smiling. Drew was sitting on Gerald's lap, one pudgy hand lifted up and placed on his father's cheek. He couldn't have been more than two. Dimly he remembered there had been some happy times. But the memories were faded, and sometimes he wondered if he'd only imagined them.

And Gerald had kept the picture hidden away in a drawer, like a dirty secret. Drew put it down on the dresser's surface and stepped back. "I don't remember it," he murmured.

"Then consider it a gift," she replied softly. "A real reminder that there were some good times. Look at the light in Gerald's eyes. He loved you, Drew."

Drew tried to hide a telltale sniff and turned away, so she wouldn't see how her words had affected him. "Let's do the closet next, okay?"

He opened the closet door, immediately hit by the scent of Gerald's aftershave. He closed his eyes as the spicy smell enveloped him. For a moment it was almost as if Gerald was there with him. He reached out and touched a flannel shirt. The cotton was worn and soft beneath his fingers, and tears stung the backs of his eyes. Gerald would never wear it again. He would never be back, and Drew would never have the chance to ask him all the things he'd wanted to. He was gone, his death a cruel and final blow to their estrangement.

"Let's take them off the hangers, Drew." Jen's voice was near a whisper as she placed her hands over his, gently slipping the top button out of the hole and sliding the shirt off into her hands. Her gentle encouragement kept him going until all that was left was the hollow tinkling of the hangers on the rod.

"There's a box up top. Can you reach it?"

Drew looked up, seeing a curious plain brown box, the kind that boots came in. He reached up and slid it off the shelf.

"Let's take it to the bed and open it," Jen suggested as Andrew wiped a thin film of dust from its surface.

They sat on the edge of the bed with the box between them. Carefully Andrew slid the tabs from the slots and lifted the cover.

What was inside sent his heart racing. Not the boots he'd expected, but clippings, letters, pictures. With trembling fingers he sorted through them, although they were meticulously organized. All the letters he'd mailed and never had a reply to, the envelopes opened and the pages wrinkled from frequent handling. Newspaper clippings, the paper yellowed but each one a highlight of Andrew's veterinary career both in Canada and in the U.S. His graduation announcements. It was all there.

"Drew?"

He realized several minutes had passed, and Jen was there, simply waiting for him. He reached out and took her hand. "He cared. He really cared."

"Yes, he did."

He looked up at her and saw her eyes were brimming with

tears. He blinked and released her fingers, wiping his hand over his face.

"What's in the bag?" She nudged him on, picking up a small cloth bag tied with a drawstring.

With a deep breath he untied the fastening and turned the bag out on top of the papers.

Glittering white stones tumbled into the box, clattering loudly in the reverent silence. Andrew stared at the misshapen lumps, picked one up in his fingers, turning it over.

"What is it?"

"Quartz." He caught his breath after saying the single word, fighting to keep his composure.

"Why quartz?"

He closed his eyes, took a deep breath. This was Jen. She'd stuck with him throughout the whole afternoon. He could get through this part.

"When I was a boy we had a game. We would find quartz and keep the brightest pieces. Gerald told me that quartz was supposed to bring wealth and prosperity. I kept all the best ones in a shoebox in my room." He paused, his stomach sinking with guilt. "I threw them all away the day I left. But he...he carried on, didn't he? Without me." His voice broke at the end. Here was the proof he had been sure didn't exist. Seeing it, touching it, had caused the dam to finally break. Clutching the stone in his hand, he lowered his head and cried.

Jen slid the box backward on the bed, moved over and knelt on the quilted spread, putting her arms around him. For a few minutes he simply let himself grieve. And when the worst was over he pulled her down into his lap and held her close. She had always believed. He was profoundly grateful she'd been here with him today. That he hadn't had to go through it alone.

"I wasted so much time," he murmured when he was back in control. "I should have come sooner. Why didn't he ever write back?"

Jen shook her head as it rested on his shoulder, releasing the scent of her shampoo, something light and feminine and familiar. "I don't know."

"I'd trade all my money for one more afternoon searching for rocks with him."

Her arms squeezed around his middle and she turned her face up to his. She'd been crying too, and in that moment he felt closer to her than he ever had.

"Why don't we? Let's go find some. You and me. Where was the best place?"

The idea suddenly sounded brilliant, and he smiled. "The creek bed by the west pasture."

"Wonderful. It's a beautiful spring afternoon. Take me there. It's been so long since we wandered the fields. We'll find new stones, and you can show me where you've pastured the rest of the herd. Tell me your plans."

He nodded, sliding her off his lap and standing. "We can leave the rest for later." The idea of being outside in the air and the sun grabbed hold. "Do you have a jacket? It's cooler today, and there's a cold front on its way."

As Andrew grabbed his jean jacket from a hook, Jen retrieved her coat from her car—a blue-on-blue nylon jacket that kept out the wind. Together they set off to the west and the far quarter section, where Andrew had pastured the healthiest members of the herd. The creek ran through the middle. The horses would be undisturbed there, with acres of luxurious grass to graze on and room to run and be free.

When Jen thought of the cramped quarters they'd endured in the transport truck, she couldn't help but feel happy for the animals in their new life. And proud of the man who had made it happen. A man who had finally found a measure of peace this afternoon. She pushed back the tiny voice of caution in her head. She would not listen today. Today was about more important things.

They walked in silence, but each footstep they made somehow drew them closer together, as if their hearts were speaking though their tongues were quiet. Jen was taken back by a startling sense of déjà vu, of afternoons when, as teenagers, they'd walked this very path just for precious moments alone.

She had memories of that time, bittersweet ones, of the intensity of young love and how much it had hurt knowing it was over. Walking those paths again, she realized that they were not the same people. They were Jen and Drew *now*. Jen felt the reassuring presence of him walking beside her and remembered how he'd kissed her the night of the dance, how he had held her just this afternoon, how he had turned to her when he needed help. She would have fallen for him anyway. It was the new Drew that had recaptured her heart.

Drew's boots made scuffing sounds in the dirt as he ambled along beside her, and their elbows bumped. Nerves of anticipation quivered through Jen's belly as Drew clasped her hand in his. Today they had turned a page, and she no longer knew what was ahead for them. She only knew it was different from anything that had gone before.

They finally reached the far gate of the section, and Jen sighed as he slid the latch open and they went inside. "Oh, Andrew. I'd nearly forgotten how beautiful it is here."

The mountains spread out in a white-capped line as far as she could see to her right and to her left. This section of fencing sat atop a small rise, so that more of the foothills lay before them, the density of the trees increasing until they formed a solid greenish black line against the gray stone. To their right she could hear the faint gurgling of the creek.

"Me too." He kept her hand in his and she squeezed, turning her head to look up at him. He squeezed back. "The first time I felt like I was really home was when I came out here."

"Do you still wish you'd never come back?" She held her breath, waiting for the answer. Coming out here today marked something important: a willing sharing of time together simply for the purpose of being together.

"Not after today. Today changed a lot of things."

"The good times…what do you remember?"

He pulled with his hand, so that her body jostled the side of his. "You. Being here with you. How you'd bake us cookies on a Saturday afternoon and we'd go for walks like we are today. Hanging out with Noah and having him sneak me a beer when I was underage. That sort of thing."

"The not so good times—they have to do with Gerald, don't they?"

He pulled his hand from hers and took a few steps away. He nodded; she saw the back of his cowboy hat rise and fall along his neck.

"We were so angry at each other. We never managed to be on the same page. For a while I thought it was just typical teenage 'he doesn't understand me' stuff. And then when he told me I wasn't his I thought I had it all figured out. I held on to that resentment for a long time. And now I'll never be able to ask him about it. Finding that box today made me realize I was the one with the closed mind. I don't like that about myself very much."

They followed the sound of the creek and stood on the rocky bank, watching the gray water bounce and race over stones.

Jen knelt, trailing her fingertips into the frigid water. "You are very much like him, you know. In good ways, strong ways. I think if he pushed you it was because he wanted good things for you. He accepted you as his son, I know he did. I think he wanted you to accept him as your father."

Andrew reached down and picked up a crystal-white stone, holding it up to show her. She smiled, and he tucked the rock into his pocket and hunched his shoulders against the rawness of the wind. "I did. I always did. I wouldn't have wanted him to understand so much if I hadn't."

Jen went to him and laid her cheek against his back. It was a comforting place to be, secure in his warmth and strength. "You deserved to know the truth, Drew. It is unfortunate that it came to light in anger. And it is sad that it caused so much regret for everyone."

The wind picked up, and tiny sharp snowflakes started dotting the air around them. Jen looked up, surprised to see how quickly the dark cloud that had been to the northwest had closed in. She shivered in her coat and put her fingers in the fleece-lined pockets.

Drew mirrored her movements. "I can't change what's past, as much as I'd like to. I have to look forward. I set up this project and I'm committed to it. It's a lot of work. I'm not playing at ranching."

Jen pursed her lips, wondering how on earth he could be so blind. She had feelings for the man he'd become. But she realized he was still stuck in the past, and she wondered if when he looked at her he saw the girl she'd been or the woman she'd become. She wanted him to see the new Jen. The Jen who had been shaped by the past and had built herself a good life. That was the woman she wanted him to care about, not the girl he'd left behind.

"I go through the same thing with my business. People act like it's some sort of hobby when I put in longer hours than most people with regular jobs." She looked up at him, hoping he would understand her side of it. "And with you too. We grew up. But people think that because we were high school sweethearts we'll just pick up where we left off."

"But that's not true."

She shook her head. "How can it be, when both of us have changed so much?"

Drew looked into her eyes, grayish blue and questioning. She had changed. She was stronger than before. More beautiful. His gaze dropped to her lips, full and red against her flawless skin. More stubborn too. She hadn't given up on him. And, while it had gotten him through today, there was still a part of him that wondered if she didn't expect too much.

"So why *are* we here?" he asked, not moving any closer to her, but feeling a sense of contact just the same.

"I..." But her voice faltered and she lowered her lashes. Andrew's heart bumped against his ribs.

His lips curved up just the slightest bit as he closed the remaining gap between them and tipped up her chin with a finger. Delicious color bloomed in her cheeks and he thought about kissing her in the barn. "I know why I'm here."

A small laugh bubbled from her lips. "You're impossible." She shivered suddenly. "And it's got cold fast."

The snow had started coming down harder. A thin layer settled on the green blades of grass. He should have known that word of a cold front didn't mean anything. Spring snowstorms were common, and by the bite of the wind this one was settling in to stay. Meanwhile, they were a long way from the house at Lazy L. And he'd been standing here staring into her eyes like a fool, hoping to God she didn't expect too much out of him at the same time. What a damn mess.

"We need to get back, Jen." The weather was suddenly more important than feelings. "This isn't going to blow through."

He saw her shiver, and chafed her arms with his hands. She was only wearing light sneakers on her feet, no gloves, and just a T-shirt beneath her jacket. "Come on, we've got to get moving. The way the wind's coming up, you're going to be frozen by the time we reach the house."

They were only about halfway back and his toes were cold in his boots; Jen's had to be freezing. Her hair was coated with snow, and she walked briskly with her arms wrapped around herself. He stopped them, brushed her hair off with his hands and took off his hat, settling it on her head. At least it would keep her a little bit dry, and he took her hand as they set out again.

At a fork in the road he made a decision. "Jen, it's coming down fast, and it's too far to the house." He cursed himself for getting caught up in their time together and not seeing the signs in the clouds. He'd thought it would be hours before they'd see any significant weather. "I have an idea."

She looked up at him, her teeth chattering. "The shack?"

"Yes. It's only around that bend, and we can wait out the snowfall."

"Can't someone come and get us?"

"Yes, but not until after the snow stops." He looked past her shoulder. The flakes were larger now, and coming down in a thick blanket. "The visibility is terrible. But it's May. It won't last that long. Okay?"

She nodded, and he felt relief fight with anxiety. He hadn't forgotten the other night in the barn, and how close he'd been to taking things further. How much he'd wanted to. But there was no time to think of those things now. The storm was worsening and they were getting too cold. They had to get out of the elements.

"Come on," he called against the wind, and tugged her hand. They jogged down the vee in the path and around a bend beyond some straggly spruce trees.

They took the snow-covered steps at a trot, and Andrew lifted the iron latch on the door. He gave it a shove with his shoulder and the wood gave way with a creak. They stumbled inside, shaking their clothes and shuddering against the cold. Jen took off his hat and placed it on an old table; Andrew stomped his feet and looked around him.

He'd been out here a few times already. The first time he'd been working on the shelters, and curiosity had gotten the better of him. The door had stuck, as it always had, but the place had been neat but dusty. Someone had kept it up during the years he'd been gone. The memories had caught him from every corner as he'd taken the rugs and blankets and aired them out over the rickety rail outside the door. At the time he'd wondered why he was doing it. Now he knew. This shack was going to keep them comfortable while they waited out the storm.

But it wouldn't keep them safe from the desire that kept flaring between them. Or the fact that they were going to be alone for several hours with precious little to keep them occupied.

"I'll start a fire," he said quietly, slipping back out into the snow for an armload of wood.

Jen watched him through the dusty window, tramping across the clearing to a rudimentary lean-to holding wood already split. In the sudden fury of the storm the shack had seemed a wonderful reprieve. But now that they were here it was different. The intimacy of it was threatening. Who knew how long they would be here? The day had started out as carefree and easy. Now they were stuck together, assaulted not only by memories but by the events of the afternoon and their blooming attraction.

As she watched, her fingers curled into her palms, Andrew reappeared, carrying an armload of wood and a hatchet. She hurried to open the door for him, letting in a blast of cold air.

"Thanks." He opened the small woodstove and arranged several sticks, then took the hatchet and began chipping off strips for kindling. When he had it all to his liking, he opened a small tin box and took out matches. Within a few seconds the beginning of a fire was crackling.

"Can you watch this? I want to get more wood before the snow gets deeper."

Jen's unease multiplied. Surely they weren't going to be here that long? Reason warred with sudden panic. She'd seen this kind of storm often enough this late in the year. One odd system coming over the mountains that brought a sudden burst of heavy wet snow. Not flurries, but a full-on storm. One that wouldn't be over in an hour. And soon it would start growing dark, eliminating the possibility of rescue until daylight.

She added a stick to the fire, sighing. The taking it slow, one day at a time principle was about to be blown to pieces. She was pretty sure that spending the night in a secluded one-room cabin wasn't taking things slowly.

Drew came back in three more times, constructing a neat stack of wood along one wall that should keep their fire going for several hours. When he was done, he rubbed his hands in front of the stove while Jen sat at the drop-leaf table in a chair that had been cast off from the main house.

"So now we wait?"

"Yep."

Warmed, Drew stood and made a trip to the cupboard. First he took out several candles and stuck them in tin holders. He lit them one by one, the flickering glow adding a homey touch to the rough setting. Returning to the cupboard, he pulled out a teakettle, a tin, and two mugs, depositing the lot on the table with a grin.

"You've been in here already!" Jen's head snapped up in surprise. The candles and matches were new, and the kettle and mugs were free of the fine film of dust that coated the furniture. He couldn't have planned for the storm, but the knowledge that he'd been here since his return did funny things to her insides.

"I remembered it when I was out here building the shelters. It's been vacant for a while, but it *has* been used since…"

The fact that he let the words trail off told her where his mind had gone, and heat rushed into her cheeks. *Since we were here* was how that sentence would have finished.

"I'll fill the kettle with snow." She scraped back her chair, in a hurry to escape the warm glow of his eyes. The cold air stole her breath as she ran out and scooped snow into the kettle, then ran back in again.

He took the kettle from her and put it on the stove, the moisture on it hissing as it touched the iron top. "Take your shoes off and let your feet dry," he advised, opening the tin and putting a teabag in each cup.

She wanted to ignore him, not be told what to do, but she knew he was right, and the middle of a blizzard was no time to argue. She slid off her sneakers, putting them closer to the heat of the stove. As the snow began to melt in the kettle he moved his chair closer and lifted her legs, putting them up on his lap. She bit down on her lip. Now that they were storm-stayed, every little touch suddenly took on extra meaning.

But her toes were warming a little and she tried to relax.

"I cleaned it up a little, that's all. It's a good place to be with yourself." He looked around them, and then back into her eyes again. "And you never know when bad weather is going to crop up. A thundershower, a freak blizzard. It pays to be prepared."

But nothing had prepared her for this.

It didn't take long for the stove to heat the tiny space, and the coziness lulled them against the howling storm outside. The kettle hissed quietly as the water heated, and Drew's hand stroked her calf lightly. Jen was painfully aware of the bed behind them. Gerald had built the frame, and the mattress was an old one from the house. The first time Drew had brought her here he'd explained how his father or the hands sometimes spent nights here when it was convenient.

The last time had been just before he'd left for university, when he'd told her he'd be back.

And the times in between… She closed her eyes. She wanted him more now than she ever had then.

"Jen?"

She tried to focus on his face rather than on the fantasy she'd briefly indulged in. "What?"

He held out his hand, took hers. "It's going to be okay. We're going to be fine. These storms don't last forever. We've got shelter and a fire, and tea, and I even have a few protein bars in the tin box. It's not much, but it will at least keep us going."

A thought struck her—of the herd being out in the middle of such a storm. "What about the horses?"

He reached inside the box and took out a foil-wrapped packet. "I managed to get the shelters serviceable. They'll huddle in there together, snug as a bug. Don't worry."

But she *was* worried. "Sometimes people die in these storms."

"Yes, but they aren't stranded with a Laramie." His grin flashed at her and he patted her hand. "The water's hot. Here."

He handed her half of a protein bar and went to get the kettle. She took the rectangle and nibbled on a dense chocolate corner, wondering if he'd realized he'd referred to himself as a Laramie after all. She didn't want protein bars. And, to be truthful, it wasn't dying she was afraid of. It was the intense desire she felt and what they might do to relieve it that had her in a spin. It was as if everything was conspiring to make it happen—their growing attraction, the storm, the forced intimacy of being stranded together in a room with nothing more than a bed for decent furniture. One bed. The possibilities made her swallow thickly.

She dipped out her teabag and sipped the hot brew, feeling

its warmth radiate from her belly outward. He was so strong, so capable. She stared over the rim of her mug at him, watching his fingers as he pressed his teabag against the side of the cup before removing it to an old square of newspaper.

She wanted what they had started the other night in the barn. She wanted him. All of him. Now, in the place where they'd stumbled over their first time together. Her heart beat so loudly she was sure he could hear it over the storm.

They were not children anymore. She was a woman, with a woman's heart and hopes and dreams. And, no matter how much she protested and agreed to taking it slow, it wasn't what she wanted in her heart. She wanted him to love her. *Heart and soul, can't live without you* love her. She wanted to see his face in the morning on the pillow beside hers, and she wanted to walk the corridor of the stables with him at sunset. Realizing it left her reeling momentarily, until Drew put down his cup, watching her with a strange expression on his face.

"What is it?"

The sound of his voice jarred her out of her stupor. She placed her uneaten bar back in the wrapper on the table. This afternoon he had finally taken giant strides to getting past his history with his father. A history that had been standing in their way ever since his return. Was it possible there was room for her now too? She was terrified, but she refused to look back. Life was full of chances. She didn't want to miss out on this one. Even if it meant risking her heart in the process.

CHAPTER TWELVE

SHE stood, went around the corner of the table until she was before him, took his face in her hands and kissed him.

It was a full-on, nothing held back kiss, one filled with longing and passion and urgency, and it exploded into the tiny room, expanding into something bright and alive. Andrew's hands gripped her hips as she commandeered his head. Her fingers tangled in his hair as she abandoned any reserve she'd been holding on to. Ever since that moment he'd nearly knocked her over in the street this was what she'd truly wanted, and she poured all of her love and hopes into it.

She slid her hands down beneath the denim jacket, pushing it off his shoulders into a crumpled pile on the chair as he stood, pulling her close. Their breathing grew heavy, echoing around the space, and Jen removed her own jacket, feeling goosebumps erupt on her skin even though the fire kept the room warm.

She reached for the hem of her T-shirt and pulled it over her head, sending an unmistakable invitation. Her breasts tightened as his gaze dropped to the simple bra she wore. With trembling fingers she slowly undid the buttons of his shirt, all the while feeling as if what was left of her clothing was shrinking. The moment his shirt was untethered he stripped it off and dropped it on top of his jacket. He reached out and pulled her close, and she gloried in the feel of his skin finally against hers.

They blindly shuffled to the bed, stopping when the backs of her legs hit the frame. Jen broke the kiss long enough to turn down the blankets. The action felt so private, so intimate, that her body trembled. She was preparing for her lover. The only lover she'd ever known. The only lover she'd ever wanted.

When she turned back, Andrew lifted his hand, trailing a single finger down her cheek. "Be sure," he whispered.

"Are you?"

He nodded slowly, his gaze stopping at her lips briefly before lifting to her eyes. The gold flecks seemed to reflect the candlelight. "I have been unsure of a lot of things lately, but this is one thing I know I want. I want you, Jen."

She wanted him too, and was so tired of fighting it. Tired of worrying what people would think, tired of having to keep repairing the wall she'd built around her heart. She was tired of being careful and weighing all the options. For once she wanted to simply listen to what her heart was saying, and right now it was saying that the time for wasting her love was past.

She removed the rest of her clothes, slid between the quilts, and bade him come home.

Jen opened her eyes by degrees, adjusting to the light coming through the window. A gust of cold air had her burrowing back under the blankets. It was followed by the shutting of the door. She peered toward the foot of the bed; Andrew was adding an armload of wood to the coals left in the stove.

Tears stung the back of her nose as she watched him. Last night had been more than incredible. She'd given him her body, and, more than that, he'd given her his. As his hands had gripped hers on the pillow, images had flashed through her mind. Memories of their first time that had been branded on her so long ago they would never go away, resurrected by his strong and gentle touch. The way he'd touched her, as if she were precious. The look in his eyes at that crucial moment, the mixture of love and fear and awe of it all glowing out of his face. How she'd quietly cried simply because he had touched her body and soul and how he'd held her in his arms afterward.

She'd felt all that and more last night, held fast in his arms while the wind gusted and the snow blew around the tiny cabin. But this morning something had changed. Though she couldn't put her finger on it there was a coolness, a tension in the air that hadn't been there before.

"Good morning."

He jumped a little, then turned to face her. "I didn't mean to wake you."

She dropped her lashes, then looked up again, patting the quilts. "It's not the same without you in here."

Again the uneasy feeling crept through her as she watched his movements. He came to sit on the edge of the bed, but made no move to get back in it. She felt at a disadvantage because he was fully dressed and she was wearing nothing at all.

"The fire burned down. I had to go out for more wood."

She frowned a little. There was no intimate smile, no good-morning kiss. Was he even going to mention the little detail of them spending the night together? She said the only thing she could think of. "The snow has stopped?"

"Yes. I called Clay from my cell when I was outside. He's rounding up Dawson and some winter clothes and they'll be here in an hour."

An hour? Yesterday she'd been worried about spending too

much time shut up with him, and now it seemed precious
minutes were ticking past so quickly. She started to reach out
for his hand, then pulled back, unsure. "That's good, then."

"Yes."

Still no mention of what had happened between them.
After last night she'd expected at least a chance to be held in
his arms before the real world came crashing in again. Instead
she was faced with this stoic stranger, and uncertainty rippled
through her.

She had known being with him was a risk, but she hadn't
thought he'd shut her out completely.

"Drew, we don't have much time so I'm just going to come
out and say it." She leaned forward, holding the covers to her
chest. "Do you regret last night?"

His gaze seared her, and she reveled in the heat, clinging
to it like a beacon in a storm. "How can you ask that?"

"Because you're acting like it never happened."

Andrew looked down at her, torn between needing to
escape and wanting to climb back into the blankets with her.
He'd thought he could handle this. And last night it had
seemed so clear. But this morning he'd watched the shadows
on her face as morning dawned, watched her steady breathing, her sweet scent filling his nostrils as he rubbed her soft
hair between his fingers. Now it was complicated. He
couldn't ignore it any longer. With Jen, there was only one
choice—everything.

And everything scared him to death.

"Of course it happened, and it was wonderful." He forced
a smile, reached out and touched her cheek with a knuckle.
"But we can't stay. Surely you know that."

"We have an hour," she suggested, sliding forward a few
inches, and he felt his body respond.

"Jen..."

The smile slid from her face and her eyes dimmed. "What is it, Drew? I don't understand."

He got up from the bed and paced a few steps. "Maybe it's all too fast for me."

"You weren't running away last night."

"Where would I have run to?"

He instantly regretted the words as she slid back against the pillow, hurt etched on her face. He'd made it sound like she'd trapped him into something he hadn't wanted, and nothing was further from the truth. "I'm sorry," he added quickly. "I didn't mean it the way it sounded."

"I know. One day at a time. That was what we decided."

He looked at her, knowing from the dull light in her eyes that she was saying it because it was what she thought he needed. But he wasn't blind. Making love changed things in a relationship. Especially one like he had with Jen.

The heat from the stove began warming the air again, and Drew brought a chair over closer to the bed rather than sit next to her. He needed that space. Needed to slow things down, make her see.

"Jen," he said softly, hating that what was coming next was likely to hurt her, but knowing he had to be honest. "The truth is I'm not sure I'll ever be ready for a committed relationship, and it's not fair to you to pretend."

Jen slid out of the bed, treating him to a delectable view that nearly had him groaning aloud. She pulled on her clothes with no muss or fuss, and then in the heavy silence straightened the blankets and pillows on the bed. Almost as if they had never been there. His heart sank. He'd hurt her after all, and that was the last thing he'd wanted to do.

"Stop," he entreated, as she made her hands busy over the table. He spun in the chair. "Stop." He reached out and stilled her hands. "Would you rather I lied to you?"

"No. Of course not." She pulled her fingers out of his grasp and poured the leftover water from the kettle into the teacups, rinsing them out.

This wasn't going well.

"Will you sit so we can talk about this?"

Her head sagged, and he felt as low as he ever wanted to. And yet he knew he had to be fair. And making her believe he was something he was not was wrong. Because in the thin light of morning, seeing her head on the pillow had nearly overwhelmed him with responsibility. He'd felt the need to run.

And he wouldn't put Jen through that.

She took the chair opposite him, and when she finally looked him square in the eye he realized exactly how much damage he'd done. For the first time she looked defeated, and it was all because of him.

"Last night was wonderful," he began to explain. "But after yesterday, finding out the things I did... You don't know what it meant to me to have you there. And I got carried away."

"I believe I made the first move."

Her courage in admitting it took him by surprise. "I didn't stop you. I wanted you too. But I can't do this." He swept out a hand, encompassing them, and then dropped it into his lap again. How many mountains was one man supposed to climb, anyway? He'd had to face a lot of demons to get even to this point. There wasn't much left of himself to give. "I still have things to work through. And if I let you, you'll wait. And I don't know if I'll ever be ready. I don't want to make false promises."

"If you *let* me, I'll wait?"

Jen's harsh, bitter laugh cut through the air as she repeated his words back to him. Had he actually just said those words? Yes, she'd decided last night what she wanted, and that was every single inch of Drew Laramie. But if he thought she was going to be the pathetic girl waiting by the gate again he was wrong.

"You don't know me at all, do you, Drew?"

"What do you mean?"

Oh, he could sit there in his chair, acting all wounded and confused, but there was too much at stake now for her to back down. "You think that just because I waited for you before I'll do so again? Do you think I started my own business because I sat around and pined for you? Or planned the expansion by sitting on my thumbs?" She huffed out a sigh. "You said I wasn't the same girl that you left behind. So stop treating me like it!"

"I never said you sat on your hands. Are you honestly telling me that you would walk out this door and let me go?"

She shook her head sharply. "No. But neither would I sit around and wait."

"I'm not following." His forehead wrinkled.

Jen let out an exasperated breath as she leaned forward. "I fight for what I want these days."

Silence fell, dark and uncomfortable. And uneasy words. "Then you have changed. Because you did not go after what you wanted all those years ago. I asked you to come with me."

"You asked me to leave behind my family when we were eighteen. So we could what? Live together in some dingy apartment while you paid tuition and we scrambled to pay the rent?"

"If you had loved me…"

"Oh, you're grasping at straws now, and playing dirty." This wasn't about the past any longer. It was about the Drew that had returned to Larch Valley, and he was covering. "I could say the same words back to you. You know what your problem is? You are so bound up in the fact that Gerald did not reply to your letters! Did you ever think how he felt every time you got in touch? You were so bent on proving to him that you were right that you didn't see that it was throwing your success in his face!"

He paled, took a step back. "Don't say that."

"How would *you* feel, Drew? The son you love rejects you, rejects the farm, and rubs your nose in it by reminding you of all the ways he is better than what he left behind!"

Silence fell, heavy in the tiny cabin, and Jen already regretted the words spoken so furiously in hurt.

"I'm sor—"

But he cut her off with a wave of his hand. "Don't be. I already figured that much out for myself, so you can't make me feel any worse than I already do." His gaze gripped hers, so that she couldn't look away. "You could have gone to Lethbridge with your mum and dad. No one forced you to be stuck here. Why didn't you go with them?"

He might as well know the truth. There was nothing hidden from each other in the cold light of morning.

"I was waiting for you."

Silence fell in the tiny cabin, and a spark popping in the stove caused them both to jump. That was the simple truth she had been clinging to. She had waited, hoped he would come back every school holiday, every summer. Until she'd realized he wasn't coming and she'd got on with her life.

Jen took a step forward, entreating. "That's right. I waited rather than going after what I wanted. You want to know why this town acts so protective of me? Because they were there for me when you weren't."

She hooked her thumbs in the pockets of her jeans. "If you had told me about Gerald and how hurt you were maybe I would have reconsidered. But we'll never know. And do you know why?" She rushed on, feeling the hurt and anger pour over her in painful waves. "Because you never trusted me. You could have told me a million times about Gerald and I would have understood. I would have been there for you. But you didn't let me in. Do you know how much that hurts me? To know you thought so little of me, when I loved you with everything I had? But now I realize you've never trusted me. You came up with the benefit idea to help my business... Did you not think I could make it work on my own? You embarrassed me at the dance in an obvious effort to drum up clients, when I'm already pretty well versed on how to advertise myself. You overpaid me and I didn't say anything, because we were friends and I knew deep down that you meant well."

"I was trying to help!"

"I never asked for your help!" She shouted it, feeling her blood pressure rise, her muscles tighten as the argument built. "I built that business on my own. *I* did it. Just me. No one else. For a while I kept thinking that the whole town only saw me as half of us, but that's not true. They know exactly how hard I've worked to make the bakery succeed. Everyone in this town gets it. Everyone but you. Because to you I'm poor Jen who got left behind. Except I'm not."

She lowered her voice, but her words were deep with meaning. "I'm Jen that stayed. I'm Jen that faced her life instead of running away from it."

"Stop it," he growled, spinning away and staring out the window, his hands bound into tight fists.

But she had gone too far to pull back now. She didn't even care if he saw her cry or not. He was brushing her aside as if what they had didn't matter. "It's true. And you know what else, Andrew Laramie? You say if I'd loved you I would have gone with you. And perhaps that is my cross to bear. Maybe I did fail you. But don't ever accuse me of not loving you. I did love you. I love you now. I never stopped."

Her voice started to break but she pushed on. "I have always loved you. Even when you make me furious, even when you make me stark crazy, I'm in love with you. And you're too much of a damn coward to take what has always been yours!" She finished with her hands on her hips, the sound of her harsh breathing filling the air, hot tears streaking down her cheeks.

She sucked in a breath, trying to regain a little control. "I'm not going anywhere. Don't you get that?" She said it quietly, a whisper that filled every corner of the room.

He turned around then, his honeyed eyes dim and bleak. "But I am."

The adrenaline swept out of her body in an instant, leaving her weak and unsteady in the void. Why hadn't she seen it coming? But after the other night he'd made it clear he had too many obligations to leave again. Oh, nothing made sense. All she could think of to say was, "Where?"

He shook his head. "I don't know. But someday I will. It'll all be too much and I'll be off again. Because you're right, Jen. You're the one that stayed, and I'm the runner. It's what I do." His lip curled as he continued in a voice filled with self-hatred, "Things got bad and I took off. Just like my mother. And I won't hurt you the way she hurt all of us."

Jen rushed forward, grabbing his arm. "How can you possibly know what happened if you haven't even spoken to her in twenty-five years? You should try to find her. Get her side of the story. Finally put it all behind you." She had to convince him. She couldn't have risked it all for nothing. She couldn't let him walk out of her life again. "I'll even go with you."

"No."

His withdrawal was clear. Jen felt it open a gulf between them and knew she'd lost. Gerald didn't matter. Their night together didn't matter. He had closed himself off to her once again. She'd told herself she had her eyes wide open where he was concerned, but she had been wrong. She'd let herself hope, that was all. She'd seen what she wanted to see.

He grabbed his jacket from the foot of the bed and

shrugged it on as the hum of snowmobiles filled the air. He jammed his hat on his head and went to the door.

"Stay here. I'll be right back."

He slammed out the door, leaving her standing in the breach of stunned silence.

What had just happened?

Last night had been exalted, glorious, mesmerizing. How had they gone from that to here in the rising of a single sun?

She sank into a chair, taking deep breaths. She had to act as if everything was normal in front of Clay and Dawson. She couldn't cry. She had to pull herself together.

"Hey, O'Keefe!" A shout sounded from the ramshackle porch, and she pasted on what she hoped would pass for a smile. Clay Gregory clumped in with a backpack in his hands.

"Well, if it isn't the cavalry to the rescue." She stood up and went to take the pack from his arms.

"Brought you some winter gear, courtesy of Dawson's sister."

"And I appreciate it."

Clay's keen eyes took in the neatly made bed, the stove and the clean mugs on the table. Jen raised an eyebrow and cautioned, "Don't even."

"Did I say anything?"

"Do you ever have to?"

He laughed. "True enough."

As she took boots, gloves, hat and a ski jacket out of the pack, Clay looked closer. "You okay? Do I need to take Andrew aside? I told him to watch his step with you."

She snorted out an emotional laugh. "I'm fine. Just hungry and ready to go home."

She had to look away as she said the word home. Going back to her house, away from Lazy L, looked as if it would mean the end of her relationship with Drew. Just thinking about it felt like a crater opening up in her center.

"If you're ready, then, let's get out of here," Clay suggested.

Jen looked around the shack, made sure the stove was closed up and the damper turned. Drew wasn't even going to come back in, she realized. Swallowing thickly, she shoved her hands into the thick gloves and clumped out behind Clay to the snowmobiles.

Drew approached from the woodpile and climbed on behind Dawson without a word. Jen got on behind Clay and put her arms around his waist as he gunned the throttle. The sun was out, sparking glittering crystals of light off the new snow, and the air was growing milder by the moment as they sped back along the path toward Lazy L. At any other time Jen would have thought it a beautiful day. But not today. By tomorrow most of the snow would be gone—melted away just like her hopes for herself and Drew.

CHAPTER THIRTEEN

THE daffodils and tulips had weathered the storm, their cheerful golden blooms nodding along the edges of the fenced garden. The grass was green again, the air perfumed with spring, the resilient branches that had drooped under the weight of snow now stood strong, displaying their leaves. The potentilla and spirea were beginning to spread along the iron fencing. Gardens all through town were dark with freshly tilled soil and newly planted flowers. It was almost as if the blizzard had never happened.

Drew waited by the gate for several minutes, unsure. Finally he took a big breath and went inside. It didn't take him long to locate the stone; he'd been here for the interment the previous fall. Then the ground had been brown and dreary. Today, as he stopped by Gerald's grave, it was carpeted with green and decorated with a colorful arrangement of daisies and bluebells. He wondered briefly who might have placed them there, knowing somehow in his heart that it was Jen. She'd been a better daughter to Gerald than he'd been a son. He reached out and plucked out a single bluebell, turning it over in his fingers before tucking it into the front pocket of his jacket.

He knelt before the grave, reading the name, date of birth—

today—and the date of death. It said nothing else. The other stones nearby said "*beloved wife*," or "*cherished father*," but not Gerald's. Gerald had died probably feeling unloved. It was a horrible burden for Andrew to bear now—now when he understood and could not tell him so.

"I'm sorry," he whispered brokenly. Whispering was the only way he could form words; his vocal chords were constricted, prohibiting true speech. He reached out and placed a hand on the cold granite, wondering somehow if Gerald could hear him, wherever he was. He wanted to think so, wanted to think that somehow his father knew he was here. That somehow, beyond his understanding, perhaps it didn't have to be completely too late.

"I was wrong and I was stubborn. It wasn't your fault."

He stared a long time at the stone, long enough for the sun to disappear under clouds, for the air to lose its benevolent warmth. Gerald had never treated Noah any differently than himself. He had simply been a man unused to sharing his feelings. Drew had been so blind. So he knelt, making peace, asking for forgiveness. When he could manage it, he cleared his throat. "You were a good father, Dad. I know I disappointed you. I hope you're proud of me now."

But he knew that while Gerald would have been glad to see him come home, he'd have been disappointed in how Drew had treated Jen. She had walked out of his life, just as he'd wanted her to. Because he'd been too afraid to reach out and accept what she was offering. Too afraid of failing her to trust in her love.

He'd all but ignored his brother too, the one person he'd always counted on in childhood. The phone call this morning had sent him reeling. Noah was in hospital. He'd been wounded in action, and was recuperating in Germany until he could be sent home.

But leaving Jen that morning in the cabin had made him face a lot of ugly truths. One being that he was following a pattern of hurting the people he loved most and then hating himself for it. Gerald, Noah, Jen. He looked down at his father's grave and knew he could never take back the things he'd said and done, could never change the years he'd wasted. But he could look forward. He didn't have to be doomed to making the same mistakes. He knew that now.

He was tired of making the wrong choices, trying to prove the wrong things. Even a few days without her had been empty and pointless. The loneliness had given him the courage to take the final step.

He reached into his coat pocket and withdrew the lump of quartz he'd picked up that day at the creek and he placed it next to the daisies and bluebells. Then he pushed up off the ground and brushed at the damp dirt on the knees of his jeans. He swiped at his eyes, kissed his fingertips and pressed them to the top of the stone.

"Happy Birthday, Dad," he whispered. As the first raindrops fell, he turned his back and made his way back out of the gate.

Jen hurried back along Main Avenue, hustling her way between bank and bakery through the rain that had sprung up so suddenly. She'd met with the realtor and a "For Sale" sign now hung outside Snickerdoodles. She'd hated watching the stake going into the ground, but knew inside that a Larch Valley with Andrew in it wouldn't work. He could say all he wanted about leaving, but Jen knew he was committed to Lazy L. As long as he remained, she would never be able to move forward, to be happy. But the decision, and every step toward the day she would leave, was ripping her heart to shreds, strip by strip.

She slowed briefly, allowing a young mum with a toddler to

skirt past and into a storefront. And then there he was. Standing across the street, hair dripping, his oilskin jacket beaded with rain. Her feet stopped as their eyes clashed, as her heart leapt at the simple sight of him. This was why she had to go.

A splash of blue caught her eye, right there in his breast pocket. She knew even from this distance that it was a blue-bell. He had been to his father's grave. He knew she had been there. Her lip quivered. She didn't want any of this. She didn't want to sell the bakery, she didn't want to leave Larch Valley, and she didn't want this distance. And still he gazed at her as her eyes filled, bereft by the gulf between them.

Drew saw her standing there, soaking wet in the rain, and his heart went into overdrive. In the space of a second the "For Sale" sign over her right shoulder registered. The bakery was up for sale. But the bakery was everything to her! Had he pushed her out of her home, then? Had he hurt her that much that she couldn't stand to be near him any longer? He pushed away the sense of guilt and shock. There was no time for that now.

He couldn't lose her. Not now when he'd finally put it all back together. Gerald. His mother. And her. It all made sense. But the pain in her eyes tore at him. At what cost? It couldn't be too late. He wouldn't let it be too late.

And then her lip trembled. He stepped off the curb toward her, mindless of traffic and rain. For the space of a heartbeat she hesitated, then her feet moved…one step after another… her gaze locked with his. They met in the middle of Main Avenue, moved straight into each other's arms. Their mouths clashed, a meeting of despair, hurt, apology and hope, cold with the wet of the rain and heated by the strength of love.

And when he finally took his lips from hers he closed his eyes and simply held on.

"I love you."

* * *

Jen's heart rejoiced and wept at the same time. Oh, just when she thought she couldn't cry anymore, that did it. Those three little words caused her to become completely undone inside, flooded with love and utter relief. She sobbed into his jacket, her fingers curled into the stiff fabric.

His soft chuckle sounded in her ear. "Shh, it's okay," he murmured. Then quieter, stronger. "It's going to be okay."

She struggled to stop crying. There was a shushing sound, and then a loud beep as a car swerved out around them. "We're in the middle of the street." His voice was a sexy rumble that she'd never get tired of hearing.

"I don't care."

"People are probably staring."

"Let them," she decreed, and his arms closed tighter around her.

He put his hands on either side of her head, kissing her forehead tenderly. "Yes, but I have things to say, and in the middle of Main during a spring shower wasn't what I had in mind."

"My house." Jen stepped back, touched his face and took his hand. "It's the only place we'll get any privacy."

They ignored the curious faces of neighbors and strangers on the street and took two left turns, heading northwest into the residential part of town. When they got to the gate of Jen's house Andrew paused. "I haven't been here since…"

"It doesn't matter. Not anymore."

She unlocked the door and they stepped inside. For a few awkward moments they took off their wet coats and shoes, ordinary movements in a day that was anything but usual. Still in the tiny foyer, he looked down into her eyes. "I want to kiss you again."

"No one is watching." She smiled a little then, a slight tease, stepping into his embrace. His fingers found the elastic holding her hair in its tail and he slid it out. Then he plunged his hands into the strands, cradling his head as he kissed her...and kissed her...until they'd had enough to satisfy them. For now.

"Tell me again."

"I love you."

She swallowed thickly, determined that her earlier tears were the last of the day. "You're sure?"

He squeezed her hand. "I've never been more sure of anything in my life. I saw your face across the street and I just knew. This is home. *You* are home."

He lifted her fingers and kissed them. "Come sit, and I'll explain everything."

She followed him into the living room, the one she'd completely redone after her parents had moved. No more eggshell paint and floral furniture. The walls were a honeyed brown, the sofa and chairs a rich chocolate. Drew sat on the sofa and drew her down on the cushions beside him.

"You went to see Gerald today."

"Yes. But I wasn't the first. You left the flowers, didn't you?"

She nodded. "This was the first year I didn't make him a cake, you know. It felt sad when I got up this morning."

"I realized something today. You were a good daughter to him, even though he wasn't your father. And I need to thank you for that. Because without you he would have been alone."

"Blood isn't the only thing that ties families together, Drew."

"I know. And sometimes blood isn't enough to hold them, either. I was wrong. And I can't go back and fix it. I thought running from it would make it go away, but it didn't. In all the ways that counted, Jen, he *was* my father. And I'm ashamed of how I treated him and ashamed of how I treated you. You were right. I didn't trust you. I was too afraid. You said you loved me. But my mother said that too and she left.

Gerald never said it, and when he revealed I wasn't his son I thought I understood. I was so afraid you'd leave that…"

Jen sighed, feeling her heart break for him. "You left me first."

He nodded, looked down at their joined hands. "I thought you saying you wouldn't go with me was the proof I needed. And when you told me you loved me again, the only thing I knew was that I would end up hurting you again. Because that's what I do. I leave. I hurt people and I leave. Like my mother did."

She slid closer, rubbed a hand over his back. "Don't you know by now you are safe with me?"

"I went to see my mother. You were right about that too."

"Oh, Drew." She lifted his fingers and kissed them. "I'm so sorry for what I said that morning. About how you hurt Gerald. About everything."

Andrew looked down at her bent head, feeling nothing but love for her flooding through him. "I kept working—kept trying to show him that I was worth it, you know? I never thought about how else it might seem. Like I was throwing it in his face."

"I'm sorry I said that." Jen looked up at him with the smoke-gray eyes he loved so much, not judging, just accepting.

"No, you were right. I couldn't put it back together until I had all the pieces. So I went to see her."

Andrew held her close, needing to feel her next to him. The trip hadn't been easy, even if it had been necessary. Julie Laramie—Julie Reid now—was a shell of a woman who'd never found the happiness she'd looked for. There hadn't been room in his heart to be angry. All he'd felt was pity.

"She's living in an apartment. Divorced again. She looks old and tired, like a faded ghost of a woman."

"Do you want to help her?"

He sighed. "I doubt she'd accept my help. She hasn't had

an easy life, Jen. She told me why she left." He sighed, remembering the bitter woman who'd smoked cigarette after cigarette in her kitchen when he'd gone to her for answers. "She wasn't happy with him. She said she tried but that it wasn't working, and that she'd had an affair. The affair produced me. Things never got better with them."

"He never forgave her?"

"I'm not sure now it was about forgiveness. He wasn't as hard a man as I convinced myself. He wouldn't have tried again if he hadn't loved her, you know? He just didn't have the words." He reached out and touched her cheek with a finger. "I don't want to be like that. I want you to know how I feel."

"Oh, Drew," she sighed, closing her eyes against the gentle touch of his fingertip.

"But when she stepped out again Gerald put a stop to it. The sad thing of it is, Jen, in her way she loved him. I could tell. She kept saying that he was a good man, that it was her fault. How can I hate her for that? How can I possibly judge when I've made so many mistakes of my own?"

Jen curled her legs beneath herself, leaning up against him so that their two bodies only took up one third of the sofa. "I'm so sorry, Drew."

"He was a good father, and she knew it. He told her he was keeping *his sons*." The words were flavored with regret. "She said she didn't fight for us because she knew he was right. That we would have a better life with him than with her. He wanted both of us. *He* didn't want to split us up. And I shut Noah out too, because we were only half-brothers. Now he's—"

When he stopped abruptly, she squeezed his hand. "He's what?"

"He's been wounded. I got a call this morning. They didn't tell me much except he'll be okay. But if there's one thing I'm sure of it's that he's going to have a place to come home to."

Jen sighed, and a new worry settled in her chest. Noah had been like a big brother to her—a strong, laughing young man.

He shook his head, stroked her hand. "My mother spent her life looking and looking and coming up empty. I don't want to be like that, Jen." He cupped her face in his hands. "I don't want to look beyond what's right in front of me just because I'm scared. I'm not like her."

"No, you're like Gerald. You love strong and you love deep."

"I was so wrong. I should have believed in you all along. You were so right. About everything." He tucked her head under his chin. "It's not too late, is it? Please don't say it's too late. Don't sell the bakery. You can't sell it. It means everything to you."

Jen turned then, sliding up and back until she was sitting on his lap, in the shelter of his strong arms, feeling his heart beat against her palm as she had the night they had waltzed. She looked into his eyes, the hazel eyes she'd adored half her life, and shook her head. "Not everything. It was too difficult to think of a life here without you in it. I would wither away, Drew. And I thought we were over for good. How could I stay? I needed a reason."

He gazed into her eyes and she saw in them what she'd hoped to see that morning in the cabin. "I haven't stopped loving you in nearly fifteen years," she stated with a wistful smile. "I'm not likely to stop now." She drew a line along his bottom lip with her thumb. "Your heart is safe with me, Drew."

"Then it's yours. I'm yours. Heart, body and soul, if you'll have me. Is that reason enough?"

She blinked back tears—no, she would not cry anymore today! But his own eyes gleamed suspiciously as he cupped her hand and pressed it to his cheek.

"Have all of me, Jen. Marry me."

"You and Lazy L?"

"Yes, I'm afraid you'll have to put up with my strays and unwanteds." His lips threatened to smile.

"Snickerdoodles?"

"We'll take down that stupid 'For Sale' sign the moment after you say yes."

"Babies?"

His Adam's apple bobbed as he swallowed, the green bits of his irises lighting as the smile widened. "Lord, woman—of course. Your babies. *Our babies*."

She threw her arms around his neck. Okay, so maybe she wasn't going to keep her promise not to cry again, but proposals like this one didn't come along every day.

"Is that a yes?"

"Yes. *Yes*!"

His arms came around her hard, rejoicing, clinging, renewing. Finally the grip eased into one of comfort, strength, acceptance.

"Jen?"

"Hmm?" She hummed it into the hollow of his neck, where her head rested against him.

"Tell me again, Jen."

"I love you, Drew."

He let the words wash over him, knew he'd repeat them every day of his life now that he had her in his arms. He kissed the top of her head and closed his eyes.

"I love you, too."

Do you have a forbidden fantasy?

Amanda Bauer does. She's always craved a life
of adventure…sexual adventure, that is. And
when she meets Reese Campbell, she knows he's
just the man to play with. And play they do. Every
few months they get together for days of wild sex,
no strings attached—or so they think….

Sneak away with:

Play with Me

by LESLIE KELLY

*Available February 2010
wherever Harlequin books are sold.*

---

red-hot reads

HARLEQUIN *Presents*

Sold, bought, bargained for or bartered

He'll take his...

Bride on Approval

Whether there's a debt to be paid,
a will to be obeyed or a business
to be saved...she has no choice
but to say, "I do"!

PURE PRINCESS,
BARTERED BRIDE
by *Caitlin Crews*
#2894

Available February 2010!

REQUEST YOUR FREE BOOKS!
2 FREE NOVELS PLUS 2
FREE GIFTS!

HARLEQUIN® *Romance*®

From the Heart, For the Heart

YES! Please send me 2 FREE Harlequin® Romance novels and my 2 FREE gifts (gifts are worth about $10). After receiving them, if I don't wish to receive any more books, I can return the shipping statement marked "cancel". If I don't cancel, I will receive 6 brand-new novels every month and be billed just $3.84 per book in the U.S. or $4.24 per book in Canada. That's a savings of 15% off the cover price! It's quite a bargain! Shipping and handling is just 50¢ per book in the U.S. and 75¢ per book in Canada.* I understand that accepting the 2 free books and gifts places me under no obligation to buy anything. I can always return a shipment and cancel at any time. Even if I never buy another book, the two free books and gifts are mine to keep forever.

116 HDN E4GY   316 HDN E4HC

Name _____ (PLEASE PRINT) _____

Address _____ Apt. # _____

City _____ State/Prov. _____ Zip/Postal Code _____

Signature (if under 18, a parent or guardian must sign)

Mail to the **Harlequin Reader Service:**
IN U.S.A.: P.O. Box 1867, Buffalo, NY 14240-1867
IN CANADA: P.O. Box 609, Fort Erie, Ontario L2A 5X3

Not valid for current subscribers to Harlequin Romance books.

**Are you a subscriber to Harlequin Romance books
and want to receive the larger-print edition?
Call 1-800-873-8635 today!**

* Terms and prices subject to change without notice. Prices do not include applicable taxes. Sales tax applicable in N.Y. Canadian residents will be charged applicable provincial taxes and GST. Offer not valid in Quebec. This offer is limited to one order per household. All orders subject to approval. Credit or debit balances in a customer's account(s) may be offset by any other outstanding balance owed by or to the customer. Please allow 4 to 6 weeks for delivery. Offer available while quantities last.

Your Privacy: Harlequin Books is committed to protecting your privacy. Our Privacy Policy is available online at www.eHarlequin.com or upon request from the Reader Service. From time to time we make our lists of customers available to reputable third parties who may have a product or service of interest to you. If you would prefer we not share your name and address, please check here. ☐

Help us get it right—We strive for accurate, respectful and relevant communications. To clarify or modify your communication preferences, visit us at www.ReaderService.com/consumerschoice.

HRI0